Toad

SIN CITY MC OAKLAND

SIN CITY MC

DARIE MCCOY

Edited by: All That's Wright

Cover Art/Design: Charli Childs

ISBN

Print: 978-1-961999-05-3

Ebook: 978-1-961999-04-6

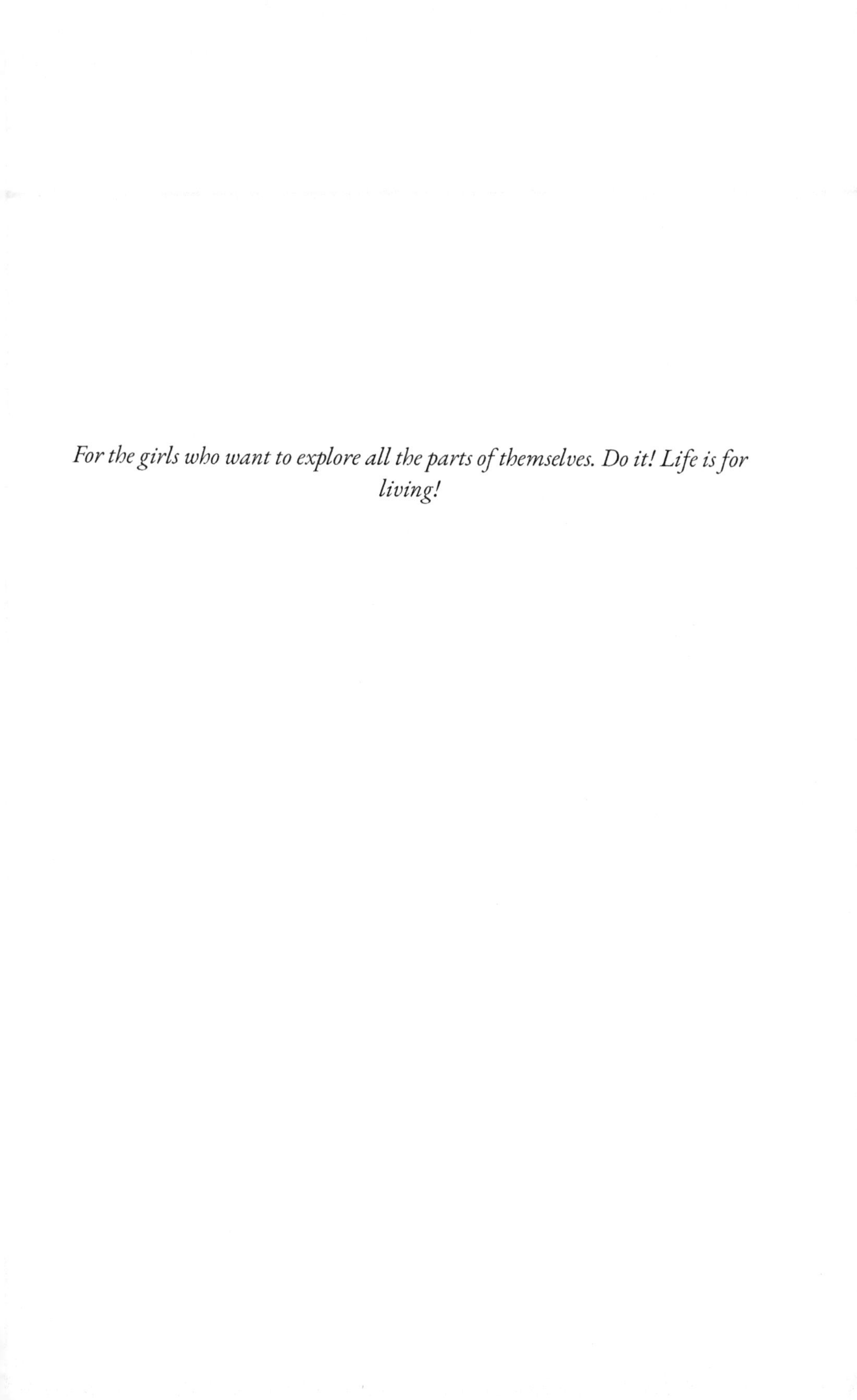

For the girls who want to explore all the parts of themselves. Do it! Life is for living!

Chapter One

People say you can't miss someone you don't know. That's bullshit. Toad missed his brother every day, even though he was only two years old when Gunn died. His MC brothers filled some of the void, but no one could close the chasm completely.

He had few real memories of Gunn aside from the ones his parents fed him through showing him pictures of the two of them together. His brother, not much bigger than Toad, was trying to hold a baby in his arms. According to their parents, Gunn was extremely protective of Toad and always wanted to help their mother care for him.

The flashes came at different times of day. Sometimes it was as soon as he opened his eyes. At other times, it was when he performed some innocuous task, or a club member asked him a question, catapulting him back to his formative years in rural Georgia.

Today, it was when he was re-racking weights someone had left on the mats instead of putting them back in their proper place. He was technically done with his workday, but he decided to get in a quick workout.

The scent of peaches wafted by, leaving him transfixed with a forty-pound weight dangling precariously in one hand. Peaches had been his and Gunn's favorite fruit. Again, knowledge given to him by his parents through pictures of the two of them. One of the last photos they had together was of the them with their round, childish faces covered in the evidence of their enjoyment of the sweet fruit.

Lifting to his full height, he scanned the area around him for the source of the scent. Equipment clanged as members lifted and lowered weights on the various machines. He used the same cleaning service as the MC. Keisha, the woman who ran things, managed to keep the normal scent of sweaty, unwashed bodies from dominating the gym.

Which was why he was able to trace the memory invoking scent to the guest being escorted by Coral, one the personal trainers on staff. She'd convinced him to add pole dancing to Sin Gym's offerings, and classes filled up immediately. Toad assumed the woman with her was a new addition, since the next session was scheduled to begin soon.

That thought was the only coherent one he had though, as his gaze ate up the bountiful curves of Coral's unnamed companion. Standing less than thirty feet away at the information desk, the unknown woman took a scent he'd always associated with his childhood and turned it into one which caused his cock to thicken. He was thankful for the confinement of his boxer briefs. Otherwise, he would've definitely embarrassed himself.

Not wanting to look like a perv who gawked at women in the gym, he tore his gaze away. It lasted all of five seconds. Remembering the weight in his hand, he placed it on the rack. Looking into the mirror behind the rack, he once again focused on her through the reflection in the glass.

Shit. Maybe he shouldn't have rejected the last few Angels who offered to help him take the edge off. There's no way he should be this fucking turned on by a woman who hadn't said two words to him. A woman who, in fact, had no idea he existed. She stood there talking to Coral and Jeannie, their receptionist. After Jeannie handed her a purple and black visitor's badge, the duo walked away in the direction of the studios designated for group exercise.

"Are you finally gonna ask Coral out?"

"Why, so you can cry into your pillow because she said yes to me after turning you down?"

Toad folded his arms. His biceps bulged under the fitted t-shirt with Sin Gym emblazoned across the front. Sitch stood next to him with a look of faux shock on his face.

"What? Man, you know I don't get bent over a woman. I have chicks falling over themselves for me to breathe in their direction. I'm not stressing about Coral or anyone else."

Picking up the towel he'd draped across a nearby bench, Toad tossed it over his shoulder. "Whatever you have to tell yourself to make it through, Sitch. Anyway, as I've said before, I'm not interested in Coral that way."

"Why the fuck not? She's hot."

Stretching his arms out, Toad allowed his gaze to roam over the expansive first floor of the fitness center.

"Look around, man. There are hot women everywhere. In this gym and all over the city. If hot was all it took, I have plenty of places to start other than with an employee. You know I don't like to fuck with my money."

"Yeah...and this has nothing to do with the Carmen incident?"

Toad lifted an eyebrow as he stared at Sitch. "Are we trading fuck ups now? If so, I can talk about Marianne, or should we start with Passion, the Angel you tried to lock down without making her your Old Lady."

The smirk dropped from Sitch's face. "Low blow, man. You know I really liked that chick."

"Yeah, for two whole weeks straight."

"It wasn't two weeks, fucker. It was a month."

He said it like it really made a significant difference. But, Toad guessed by Sitch's standards, either way was a long time. He was glad Coral could see through his MC brother's crap. He would hate to lose a good employee over fuck boy shit.

Brushing Sitch off, Toad walked away. Coral and her visitor were no longer in sight and he wanted to get in a workout before heading to the clubhouse. They had Church later, and he liked to be there beforehand. Being Sergeant at Arms was a big responsibility for him.

He didn't have nor want the politics the Prez, King, had to deal with. Toad preferred keeping order and looking out for his brothers. Depending on the topic, things could get pretty heated during Church. If a verbal reminder of the rules didn't work, he might have to get physical. Which is probably why some clubs called their Sergeant at Arms Enforcers. In Oakland, they had Fubar along with some others for that. Fubar came over from the mother chapter in Las Vegas. He was technically on the run, but a Sinner always had a home where other Sinners resided.

Toad dove into his workout after managing to shake the new peach scent from his nose. Bass thumped in his ears from the wireless earbuds. Finishing his last rep, he stepped forward and lowered the bar onto the stand relieving himself of his almost three-hundred-pound burden. Bartlett, one of the other trainers, stepped up to spot him.

When he turned from the station to grab his towel, he was once again assailed by the now tantalizing aroma. This time it was closer. Coral and her guest stopped to chat just shy of where he stood.

Apparently looking for his daily dose of humiliation, Sitch wandered closer. Toad knew Coral could handle herself, but he'd asked her previously if she wanted him to put a stop to Sitch's advances. She literally laughed in his face. Toad seriously didn't want her uncomfortable. She was a damned good trainer whose appointment calendar was constantly filled.

Once she set him straight on being able to handle herself. She assured him she'd let him know if anyone got out of line. Still, he watched, looking for any indicators that either of the ladies were feeling pressed.

As much shit as they did in Sin City MC, what they didn't do was anything involving forcing women or human trafficking. Sure, they had club whores—Angels. But, everyone was a willing participant in all activities. He needn't have worried about Coral.

After giving Sitch a disdainful up-down, she flipped her hand at him like she was shooing a fly and walked away with her guest in tow. As they drew closer, he couldn't keep his eyes from devouring the other woman. Toad would be the first to admit, he loved women in all the various shapes and shades they came in.

That being said, this woman's russet brown skin seemed to glow and called for his fingers to stroke it—everywhere. Stuck staring, Toad realized too late that they were approaching him. Dropping his hands, he hoped the towel he still held was enough to camouflage the thickness in his pants.

Chapter Two

Esmeralda tried not to laugh as Coral swatted the guy, who introduced himself as Sitch, away. It was no wonder he was attracted to her friend. Coral was what Esmeralda's granny called statuesque. She had curves for days and the height Esmeralda had craved for most of her youth. She'd long since adjusted to living with the five feet two inches she'd been granted. Still, she occasionally looked at Coral's almost six-foot frame and experienced a twinge of jealousy. Just a twinge.

The mirth died on her lips as Coral walked her toward a living Adonis. The man was a complete specimen. But considering the men she'd encountered since moving to California ten years ago, he probably knew it and thought the rest of the world should worship him because of it. *He was fine though.*

Coral greeted the Adonis as they drew closer. "Hey Toad. I want you to meet my friend Esmeralda. I finally got her to come take my pole dancing class instead of going to that bougie spot she's been wasting her money on."

Esmeralda allowed the comment about her current gym to roll off her as her brain stuttered over hearing the Adonis referred to as a wart-filled amphibian. Before she could command the muscles to stop, her brow dipped into a frown.

"Did you just say Toad?" Esmeralda stared at Coral in disbelief.

Coral gave a short barking laugh. "Yeah, don't think too hard about it."

The man in question extended a hand toward Esmeralda. His expression was a mix of politeness and irritation. She hadn't meant to be rude, but hearing such an attractive person called by a very unattractive nickname threw her off. Accepting his hand, she intended to give it a quick squeeze and release, but he held on to her digits. His fingers flexed against her skin before letting go.

"It's actually, Xavier. Toad is my road name."

At hearing the phrase *road name,* Esmeralda tensed slightly. Bikers had road names. While she didn't have extensive experience with motorcycle clubs, she'd encountered them back home in Las Vegas and here in Oakland through her work with Identalysis, the independent forensic contracting company she worked for. She'd helped to identify more than a few bodies of people who'd been involved in the biker lifestyle.

Esmeralda gave herself a mental shake. She had no way of knowing if Xavier was connected to one of the rough riding one percenter MCs. He could very well be a weekend warrior who only pulled his bike out of the garage to ride with his friends. They could simply be business owners—restauranteurs, accountants and such.

Tucking her hand back to her side, she nodded as she looked from him to Coral. If she kept looking at him, she might say something awkward, and she really wanted to avoid that. He was just entirely too much fine standing way too close, and she was two years into her latest drought. She normally didn't let it go so long, but the guys she'd gone out with kept cock-blocking themselves just when she was planning to knock the cobwebs off.

"Esmeralda. That's a name I don't hear often."

"I could say the same about Toad."

The near baritone of his voice sent a zing straight to her center. Shifting her weight from one foot to another, she tried to squelch the feeling. She didn't need her libido in this conversation with Coral's boss. Coral didn't introduce him as her boss, but she'd told Esmeralda who he was on their way in. Only she hadn't called him by name at the time.

When Esmeralda thought about it, Coral had never mentioned him by name when she talked about her work at Sin Gym.

As they entered, Coral simply pointed him out, standing next to the guy who flirted relentlessly with her. Bless his heart, Coral would never give him the time of day. He didn't have enough salt mixed in with his pepper to get her motor going.

Besides her desire to remain cordial to her friend's employer, Esmeralda's back was up at his comment about her name. She recognized that she was very much a black woman, and the name was typically associated with Latina women. The childhood jokes extended into college and now led to double-takes in her professional life—especially since she didn't allow anyone to shorten it or give her a nickname.

She knew her response had the slightest hint of a bite to it. His low chuckle said he'd heard it as well. Lifting his hands up as if in surrender, he smiled. It transformed his face to unreasonably handsome proportions. *Stop that shit!* He didn't heed her mental command.

"No offense intended. I was just curious how you got the name."

"My parents."

Esmeralda's response was clipped. Her top lip itched with irritation. It's not like he was actively poking fun at her, but she had to clamp her jaw and remind herself the man signed Coral's checks.

Thankfully, Coral intervened. "Okay, well. Toad, since you were still here, I wanted to introduce you to my friend. I'm trying to get her to consider changing her membership. Wish me luck!"

A bright smile was plastered across Coral's face as she looped her arm through Esmeralda's and guided her away. It took much more effort than she wanted to admit, for Esmeralda to refrain from looking back at him. One would think she'd never seen a good-looking man before. *Geesh!*

Esmeralda didn't object to Coral hustling her through the expansive lower floor until they reached the women's locker room. Once the door was closed behind them and Coral had walked the aisles making sure they were alone, she turned on Esmeralda.

"Are you okay?"

"What? Of course. Why do you ask?"

"Because you may be many things, but you're not usually rude."

Folding her arms across her middle, Esmeralda stared at her friend with one lifted eyebrow.

"What things?"

"Huh?"

"You said I may be many things. What things?"

"Esmeralda. Focus. Are you okay? Your tone suggested you were about half a second away from going off on Toad."

Shaking her head, Esmeralda denied Coral's assessment.

"No I wasn't! And what kind of name is Toad, anyway? Why does a grown ass man let other people call him by such an unattractive name? It sounds like he got it in second grade."

Stifling a smirk, Coral shook her head. "I don't know. All he's ever said was it's his road name. I didn't ask for an explanation. I don't get into Sin City business like that."

"Sin City? As in Sin City MC?"

"Yeah. You've heard of them?"

"There's a one percenter motorcycle club called Sin City in Vegas, but I didn't know they had members all the way up here."

"Well, there's a chapter here in Oakland. If I'm not mistaken, they've been around for at least ten years. Don't quote me though, because all of my information is third hand at best. I don't ask them about their business. That's a quick way to get fired, or worse."

"Worse? Are you in danger working here?" Esmeralda grasped Coral's forearm. She wasn't sure what she'd do if her friend said yes, but she was immediately concerned.

"Girl no. The only place I could probably be safer is at their clubhouse—although I've never been there. My little knowledge of biker life says the only women allowed are Old Ladies and club girls who 'service' the members."

"Service?" Esmeralda's faced scrunched. Then, understanding washed over her unhinging her jaw, leaving her mouth agape. "Oh!"

"Yeah. Oh." Coral chuckled. "Anyway, let's grab our stuff. I'm done for the day. We can get a quick bite down the street before we head home. There's still plenty of daylight left."

Nodding in agreement, Esmeralda trailed behind. Once they had their bags, they took a different path to the exit. At this rate, it would take her at least four visits to even partially learn her way around.

As they left, Esmeralda had the sensation of being watched. Looking around, she didn't see anyone paying particular attention to them. Shrugging off the feeling, she separated from Coral heading toward her vehicle. Following the tail lights of the impractical pickup truck her friend owned, Esmeralda left the parking lot and the feeling behind.

Chapter Three

The roar of Toad's Harley was muted by the noise canceling speakers built into his helmet. Pulling into his spot at the clubhouse, he secured his ride and entered the building through a side door. Hitting the stairs, he dropped his gym bag and helmet in his room, and went down the front stairs into the bar area. Music played from the speakers on the stage, but not loud enough to drown out the conversation of the few members scattered around.

Trick was behind the bar with a notepad in one hand and a stub of a pencil in the other. To be fair, the pencil was probably normal sized; it just looked like a stub in his huge hand. At six-foot four with long limbs and digits, Toad didn't encounter many men who made him feel small. Trick was an exception.

Breaking his concentration, Trick made eye contact. "Wanna pop?"

"Yeah."

A cold bottle of peach soda came sliding down the bar top, landing in his open hand. Where Toad grew up, in mostly rural Georgia, they called every carbonated beverage a coke. Trick was from Chicago. On any given day, he referred to them as either soda or pop. Most days it was pop. Either way, Toad understood.

If they didn't have Church soon, he'd have something stronger. Trick knew Toad never drank before Church, because he liked to stay sharp. He rarely had to tune anyone up when they didn't mind the rules of order, but he stayed ready. People assumed MCs were chaotic, and they sometimes were. But, there were rules and protocols that were followed. When they weren't, Toad was King's arm to remind the brothers who got out of line.

Toad plopped onto the empty stool next to Frenchie. The mostly silent Canadian transplant was arguably the brother he was closest to in the MC—despite Frenchie rarely stringing more than a few words together at a time. Presently, he was giving a *'what the fuck is your problem?'* look to one of the Angels. It was just the look as Frenchie wouldn't ever actually say the word 'fuck' out loud.

Toad recognized her as one of the new girls Kelsey had brought in. Either Kelsey didn't completely brief her on the rules, or she didn't care about following them. Frenchie was sitting with his back to the bar. The chick had one hand on his thigh while she leaned in, pressing her breasts into his side.

Knowing Frenchie was probably two seconds away from crushing the new girl's ego, feelings and spirit, Toad got her attention.

"You. Commere."

The new Angel pulled back from Frenchie, giving him a smirk that suggested he'd missed his chance. Red lipstick stood out in stark contrast to the paleness of her skin as she smiled at Toad. On a normal day, he might've found her attractive. Today, however, all he did was compare her skin and body to the lush richness of Esmeralda's dark skin and ample curves.

He stopped her advance before she could repeat her routine on him. "You're new, right?"

"Yeesss." She drew the word out with emphasis on the 's'.

"Kelsey brought you in?"

"Mhmm... I'm Lacey." She tried again to step closer, but he held up a hand.

"Did Kelsey happen to go over the rules for Angels with you?"

Twirling a lock of her long brown hair, she bit the corner of her bottom lip and looked up at him through her lashes. "Umm... I think so."

"Then why are you touching a member, and officer, in this club, without his permission?"

It was either his expression, the growl in his voice, the words or a combination of the three which caused her to pull up short in her attempts to flirt. A flush crept into her cheeks.

"Umm..."

"This is your one chance, and that's only if my brother agrees." Flicking his gaze to Frenchie, he interpreted his look of boredom as agreement.

"You are here at our pleasure, for our pleasure, but you don't put your hands or any other part of your body on a member unless he *asks* you to. ***You*** don't touch ***us***. ***We*** touch ***you. When, if, and how*** we want. That's what you signed up for.

If you can't get it through your head, you can twist your narrow ass out to the curb and thumb a ride to wherever it is you call home. Do I make myself clear?"

Toad didn't feel an ounce of sympathy when a fat tear rolled down her cheek. He wasn't there to soothe her feelings. She signed up to be a club whore. Just because they called them Angels didn't change their purpose. If they weren't bringing pleasure to a member, they needed to move the fuck along.

"If you can't talk, nod your head so I know you understand."

Jerky nods followed his command, and she turned on her four-inch heels and nearly ran from his presence. Bringing his bottle to his lips, Toad took a swallow of the fizzy drink. The flavor didn't compare to the sweetness of a real peach, but it would do in a pinch. When he looked to his left, Frenchie was staring at him.

"What? You didn't want her touching you, but you're giving me a face for telling her to skip her little ass on? You should thank me."

When all he got in response was more staring, Toad continued. "Whatever man. I saved you the hassle."

He held the bottle between his thumb and forefinger. It was nearly empty after only a few pulls. Running his tongue over his teeth, his thoughts returned to Esmeralda. He wasn't sure if it was simply her, or the mixture of the peach scent and her plush body that made it difficult for him to move on from the simple meeting.

The thing was, if he didn't plan to do anything about it, there was no point of him sitting around mooning over her like a lovesick boy. It was highly probable today was the first and last time she would set foot inside Sin Gym. Movement to his left made him look at Frenchie, who shifted on the barstool as if he was considering getting up.

"So... Today, Coral brought a friend into SG to take her pole dancing class." Placing the now empty bottle on the bar, Toad pressed his back against it. He didn't expect Frenchie to say anything, so he wasn't surprised when he wasn't prompted to continue.

"I was kind of skeptical when Coral wanted to start the classes. I know they were popular at one point, but I thought they'd run their course. But they continue to fill up."

Although he didn't speak, Frenchie's head tilted slightly. "Okay, fine. I don't really wanna talk about the success of damn pole dancing classes. I can't stop thinking about Coral's friend Esmeralda."

Running a hand through his hair, Toad expelled a huffing breath. "I don't know what the fuck is wrong with me, man. I was staring at her like a damn pervert. When Coral brought her over to introduce us, I had to put my hands and a big ass towel in front of my dick to keep her from seeing how she affected me.

What the hell is that shit? I'm not a fucking teenager. I'm a grown man. And I don't get hard-ons because a beautiful woman is within five feet of me."

Toad was thoroughly disgusted with himself. He looked over his shoulder. He didn't care if Trick heard him, but he wasn't keen on any of the other guys listening in on him at confession. Since Frenchie was the club chaplain, Toad sometimes considered the way information seemed to fall out of his mouth in the man's presence nothing short of going into the confession booth at a Catholic church. Although he wasn't Catholic and wasn't even close to being religious—despite his Southern Baptist upbringing.

When he looked back at Frenchie, the chaplain wore an expression which Toad read as questioning if he was done.

"Yeah, I'm done."

With a curt nod, Frenchie stood up, bumped Toad's shoulder with his forearm, and walked away. Toad checked his watch and saw that there were about fifteen minutes before Church started. Members were trickling in, going toward the meeting room. Tapping the bar twice to get Trick's attention, Toad pointed and walked away. He needed to get to his post next to the door.

He hoped they were going to finally talk about adding on to the club to get another meeting room. It was tighter than a tick's belly in a dog pound in the spot they used now.

Chapter Four

Esmeralda turned the mandible mold right to left until she had the correct angle to match the X-Ray on the large monitor. She'd been going through records for the past few days and this was the first set which looked promising. It wasn't identical though.

There were more modern methods of performing the task, but Esmeralda like to keep it hands on. She was very tactile in that way. The ring of the desk phone interrupted her assessment.

"Identanalysis, this is Esmeralda."

Her greeting was automatic after five years of working for the forensic analysis contractor. She remained focused on the monitor until she realized the person on the phone hadn't responded.

"Identanalysis, this is Esmeralda."

Placing the mold on the mat in front of her, she tipped the handset to view the display screen. The call wasn't internal, and there wasn't a business name displayed next to the numbers on the screen. The seconds increasing on the call time indicated it was indeed connected. Yet, she heard not even breathing on the line.

Frowning, she placed the phone back onto the base. *What was that about?* Shrugging, she went back to studying the mold. She would really prefer the actual mandible to the replica, but she'd been denied access to the physical remains of the victim.

The phone rang again, and she picked it up without looking at the display.

"Identanalysis, this is Esmeralda."

Once again, she was met with silence. Releasing a sigh, she looked at the caller ID and verified it was the same number from before. Not bothering to say anything else, she replaced the receiver and stood from her desk. When she walked out of her office, her assistant, Olga, was sitting in her cubicle typing away.

"Olga?"

Bright blue eyes looked at Esmeralda over the top of the computer monitor. "Hey, what's up?"

"The last couple of calls you put through, did they give a name?"

Olga's pixie-like face scrounged into a frown. "I haven't put any calls through to you today."

"What? I just got two calls almost back-to-back. If you didn't put them through, it means they called my line directly. I don't give my extension number out to many people."

Olga's expression remained confused. Esmeralda was certain her face mirrored her assistant's.

"They didn't say who they were when they called?"

"No. When I answered, the line was silent."

"That's weird." Olga shook her head.

"Very."

Esmeralda turned on her heel to return to her office. "I'm not sure what's going on, but I'm going to forward my phone to your desk for the rest of the day. If something urgent comes up, come and get me. Otherwise, send them to voicemail."

"Okay, boss. Will do."

Esmeralda still wasn't used to Olga calling her boss. Granted, she was technically the young woman's boss—it just felt strange. She initially didn't understand why the partners were insistent that the senior analysts have assistants. Now, after having Olga with her for the past year, Esmeralda appreciated the benefits of having someone else compile the reports.

All she had to do now was review the documents for accuracy and have them sent out to the appropriate parties. To date, it hadn't been necessary to correct anything other than the occasional typo. However, she checked anyway. At the end of the day, her name was on the information as the subject matter expert—not Olga's.

Back in her office, Esmeralda pressed the keypad to forward her calls, then returned to trying to confirm the identity of the person whose remains had been found at the base of Mount Diablo. According to the information from law enforcement, what was left of the victim's clothing didn't indicate they were there for the hiking trails. No gear was discovered abandoned in the vicinity, so they hadn't been camping either.

Clicking on the voice recorder, Esmeralda started dictating what she could glean from studying the mold.

"Based on the shape of the teeth, particularly the molars, the victim suffered with bruxism. It is difficult to conclude the severity using the mold. I need to view the physical remains to be certain..."

The rest of Esmeralda's day followed a normal routine. An alert from her phone let her know it was time to wrap up and meet Coral. After she attended her friend's pole dancing class, she finally agreed to look into membership at Sin Gym instead of the gym-in-a-box she'd used for the past few years.

It was shameful that it had taken her so long to leave. Esmeralda dragged her feet because Coral had been willing to come to her for their training sessions. Her friend finally drew a hard line. No, she wasn't exclusive with Sin Gym and could train whomever she wanted wherever she wanted, but Coral felt Esmeralda was wasting money.

After looking around at all three levels of Sin Gym, Esmeralda was forced to agree. Their facilities were much nicer, and they offered more classes as a part of the membership package than what she currently had.

By the time she was parked and ready to enter the outer glass double doors of the building, it was almost five p.m. She was barely in time for her late appointment to finish the on-boarding process. She waited patiently for the receptionist to buzz her in through the inner doors.

Looking through the glass, she didn't see anyone at the desk. Her gaze roamed the area between the two sets of doors before landing on a large photo mounted on the wall behind the reception desk. The entire staff was in the photo, but Esmeralda's eyes were drawn to the man standing front and center. It wouldn't have mattered if he hadn't been in the very front. Xavier Carmichael was hard to ignore. She refused to call him Toad, even in her mind.

Thankfully, her wait was relatively short. Coral was expecting her and stepped into the lobby area when five p.m. came and went without her being inside. Esmeralda returned her friend's broad smile as Coral pressed a button to allow her entry. First thing on the agenda would have to be obtaining an access card. She felt some kind of way about having to wait around outside.

A couple of members had swiped their way in while she waited. They didn't offer to let her in, and she didn't ask. So, she didn't know if they would've bent the rules for her or not.

"Hey girl! Come on. Jeannie called in sick today. One of the guys was supposed to be working the desk, but it appears he got distracted. Come this way to the office and we can get you set up. There should be someone in there."

When they rounded the corner to enter the office, Esmeralda's steps faltered slightly. She recovered quickly, so she hoped Coral didn't notice. She was sure the man at the desk didn't notice, because all she could see was the top of his head. His sandy blond hair flopped forward without any product to keep it swept to the back, the way it was in the image on the wall outside the reception area.

"Hey Toad, I didn't expect you to be here. I thought one of the other guys would be around to get Ezzy all signed up."

Xavier's brow dipped. "Ezzy?"

Standing, Xavier's dark eyes landed on Esmeralda, almost locking her voice in her throat. A quick internal pep talk was in order to get her vocal cords functioning properly.

"Esmeralda." She correctly firmly. Coral was on a very short list of people she allowed to shorten her name.

"Yes. I remember."

His gaze raked over her body, setting off a slight blaze beneath her skin, before returning to capture hers. Esmeralda was grateful she still wore the slacks, blouse and sensible bra she'd worn to work. Even with her double stacking her sports bras, she was certain the diamond tips of her nipples would've shown through.

The partial smirk he wore drew her attention to his full lips. Not large, but they could definitely get the job done. *Which job?* She wouldn't give that internal nugget time to grow into anything other than a passing thought. Coral's interruption was welcomed, and Esmeralda happily broke away from Xavier's stare, turning to her friend.

"Have you seen Cort? He was supposed to fill in for Jeannie. Ezzy needs to get her new member stuff done and get a badge. I had to come let her in because she was standing in between the doors waiting."

"Cort has a training session. I'll take care of Ezzy."

"Esmeralda."

"Excuse me. Esmeralda."

Although he accepted her correction, Esmeralda's insides quivered from the way he looked at her. It wasn't pervy. Anyone else would say he was strictly professional. He remained behind the desk. Although he'd stood when they entered, he didn't advance on her or crowd her space.

"Have a seat, Esmeralda. Let's get started."

Again, when he gestured toward the empty chair, he was the picture of professional and polite. But his voice made Esmeralda not trust herself to be alone with him. Despite her general aversion to bad boys, there was something about Xavier Carmichael that made her forget he was a patched member of a well-known motorcycle club rumored to have criminal ties.

Clapping her hands, Coral strode toward the door. "Alright then, I'll leave you two to it. Ezzy, come find me on the second floor after you're all checked in and changed."

"Okay."

Esmeralda stared at her friend's retreating form. Part of her wanted to run out after her, but it wasn't possible. Turning her gaze back to Xavier, she tried to ignore the way his presence took up the whole room. It wasn't a large office, but it wasn't exactly closet sized either.

Once again, he pointed to the empty chair. "Have a seat, and let me take care of you."

Polite and professional. But the sparkle in his eyes said he could take care of more than simply the paperwork to complete her membership at Sin Gym.

Chapter Five

When he decided to put in some time in the office, the last thing Toad expected was to do a new member intake with none other than Esmeralda. He wouldn't complain though—no matter how much he hated paperwork. He visually consumed every inch of her compact plush body as she finally accepted his offer of taking a seat in the chair on the opposite side of the desk.

The sweet scent of peaches he remembered from before preceded her into the space. His nostrils flared as he fought the urge to close his eyes and savor the aroma that was uniquely hers. Other people wore peach fragrances, but it didn't smell nearly as delectable as it did on Esmeralda. Steeling himself against crossing the line, he focused on the task at hand.

Picking up the electronic tablet they used, Toad grabbed the pen shaped stylus to open a new file. Normally, the new member was given the tablet and asked to fill out the questionnaire themselves. But, if he'd followed the usual routine, he wouldn't have been able to interact with her the way he wanted.

Asking the basic questions, he entered her full name and the other relevant information she supplied. Everything was moving along well until they reached the section regarding employment.

"Why do you need to know where I work?" Esmeralda shifted in her seat.

Her question surprised him. He knew she worked a straight job. Most folks who lived on the right side of the law usually didn't have a problem telling people what they did for a living. He didn't expect pushback from her on that particular question.

She gave off a good girl vibe—mostly. There was a hint of something else just below the surface. *Color him intrigued.* One eyebrow lifted as he explained.

"Some companies have incentive programs for employees and they pay a portion or all of the membership fees. If your employer has a similar program, I can submit the information to them, and get part or all of the costs covered for you."

"Oh." She sniffed primly. "I work at Identanalysis."

Toad didn't recognize the name, and the information wasn't strictly required on the document, but he was curious.

"Identanalysis? What kind of company is Identanalysis?"

"We primarily do forensic analysis."

Toad's jaw clenched and his fingers gripped the stylus so tightly, there was a danger he'd break it. A gravelly edge crept into his voice without conscious thought.

"So, you work for the cops?"

"No. We are sometimes contracted to work ***with*** law enforcement, but we don't work ***for*** them. They have their own labs."

"Tomato, to-mah-to." Toad grumbled. He couldn't believe she worked with the damn cops. Her being a borderline good girl wasn't a problem. He knew plenty of so-called good girls who were straight up freaks.

But, cops? He made it a point to stay away from them and from people associated with them. It wasn't just because of the shit they got into with the MC. The way the cops back home had mishandled the incident with his older brother, Gunn, had soured him on the institution. His run-ins with them over the years hadn't helped rehabilitate their image in his eyes.

"Um...No. It's not the same thing. Our association with law enforcement only extends as far as the contracts we work for them. We also work with archeologists and private citizens."

"Private citizens?"

"Yes. Sometimes people need answers and they can't get them from law enforcement. The system isn't set up to allow everyone to get the closure they need. And, sometimes, the answers given from official sources are wrong. That's where we come in."

Bobbing his head in acknowledgement, Toad moved on to the next series of questions on the form. He didn't want to dig into the cop aspect of her job any further. However, he still wanted to know more about her. Like what exactly did she do for Identanalysis and why had she chosen the forensics field?

Instead of yielding to the desire, he asked the remaining questions on the document then passed it to her for her signature. A quick search of the employer healthy partnership database confirmed Identanalysis did offer to pay a portion of the employee's membership fees. So, he flagged her account to send the verification letter to them to get it set up.

The printer outside the door came to life as he printed copies for Esmeralda to take with her. Standing, he walked around the desk. He was always conscious of his height and bulk around people significantly smaller than him. Habit had him moving slowly so as not to startle her.

"I'll grab the copies for you to take with you, but I can also have them emailed to you. That's if you prefer them electronically."

Toad felt her eyes on him tracking his movements as he stepped outside the doorway to get the printouts. If he wasn't mistaken, he detected a hint of attraction, but she was more skilled at hiding it than some of the women he interacted with at Sin Gym. *Good girl shit.*

"Follow me and I'll get you set up with a badge and show you to the dressing rooms."

They had a three second tug of war as he attempted to lift the bag from her shoulder to carry it for her. He won, and they walked the short distance to the green screen used to take member photos. Regardless of what people thought about MCs, Toad wasn't a total heathen. His mama had drummed some things into him which refused to die.

His woman wasn't allowed to carry things in his presence. That internal declaration almost made him trip over his feet. When the hell had

Esmeralda Upton become his woman? He wasn't in the market for an Old Lady. Besides, she was too strait-laced for him. Not to mention she had regular dealings with the boys in blue.

None of his flimsy excuses mattered. The decision had been made. The tips of his fingers pressed against her lower back as he guided her in the direction he wanted them to go. Clenching his jaw, he had a mental conversation with his dick about when it was and was not appropriate for it to plump up. Being so close to her and actually touching her, didn't help his case.

As they walked through the lower floor, he saw and felt the eyes on them. Some of the gawkers were his brothers; others were regular members of the gym. He ignored them all.

Toad liked getting his dick wet as much as the next man, but he recognized the oddity in what he was doing with Esmeralda. First, it was rare for him to be seen escorting a new member. Period—not just a woman. Second, he had her bag thrown over his shoulder and a hand at the small of her back.

He could possibly get away with carrying the bag, but the hand on her back was a clear sign of possession. Toad didn't give even half a fuck. They needed to be put on notice that she was off limits—whether she knew it or not.

"You don't have to walk me all the way to the dressing room. Coral showed me where it was last time."

"I'm sure she did, but I wouldn't want you to get lost. There are more than a few ways to get to the same place in here."

Her light giggle did nothing to calm his cock's desire to stiffen in his shorts. Toad looked at her with a raised eyebrow.

"You might be on to something. When Coral showed me around, she did take me a different way each time. This place ***is*** huge."

Toad was certain his chest was poked out like a proud peacock at her description of the gym. He took pride in what he'd built. Starting out as a bodybuilder on the natural circuit, he'd worked hard to garner a reputation that helped him get to where he was now.

They reached the door of the lady's dressing room much too quickly for his liking. For a moment, they stood there looking at one another. The awareness sparking between them made it feel like a first date instead of what it was supposed to be—a staff member showing a client the facility.

Finally allowing her to hold her own bag, he reluctantly released the straps. Stepping closer than he probably should, Toad dipped his head and tipped it to the side.

"I'll see you around, Princess Peach."

"Um... Thanks?"

Her confusion was entirely too adorable, so Toad turned on his heel and strode away before he did something she wasn't ready for.

Chapter Six

What was that about? Esmeralda watched Xavier walk away. Broad shoulders tapered down to a noticeably smaller waist. The muscle tee he wore didn't look as cheesy or cliché as it looked on other men. The butterflies jockeying for position in her stomach gave her no mercy.

He looked so powerful and confident; it did a number on her senses. Practical Esmeralda was locked behind a reinforced steel door as she visually devoured him. Since he was no longer looking directly at her, she felt free to enjoy the view.

"Girl, do you wanna be alone for a few?"

Her bag hit the floor with a thump as Esmeralda gasped and whipped around. Standing behind her was Coral wearing a knowing smirk. Stooping, Esmeralda picked up her bag and pushed the door open to the changing room.

"I have no idea what you're talking about. I was on my way in to get changed before I came to find you."

"Uh-huh. Tell me anything."

Esmeralda's eyes widened innocently. "I'm serious. I just finished the paperwork and got my badge."

Grasping the laminated card attached to the lanyard around her neck, she held it up to Coral.

"See. I'm all official now."

"Yeah...I see. I also saw you staring at Toad like he was a full course meal at a Michelin starred restaurant."

Esmeralda twisted her lips. "I was not."

Walking past the rows of lockers, she entered the first available changing booth and closed the door. She wasn't ashamed of her body, but she'd never been a fan of disrobing in front of strangers. Having not played organized sports growing up, she never lost the hint of shyness when it came to having her body exposed.

Again, she wasn't ashamed of the bounty she possessed; she just wasn't comfortable being on display. Esmeralda had long ago made peace with her large breast, big legs, ample hips and ass. Not to mention the rounded tummy which usually accompanied such generous proportions.

She exercised regularly and ate relatively healthy. This was simply the body she would have. No matter how much or little she worked out, it remained constant.

While she shed her clothes, Coral stood outside keeping up a steady stream of conversation.

"You don't have to be embarrassed. It's not like you're the first woman to look at that man like he was an all-you-can-eat buffet."

Pausing halfway through wrestling the first of the two sports bras she needed to keep her girls somewhat in control, Esmeralda looked at the closed door as if she could see her friend. An unrecognizable wave of jealousy swept over her.

"Excuse me? What does that mean?"

"It means what I said. Toad is an attractive man with a nice physique. You aren't the first woman to look at him and appreciate it."

Esmeralda bit her bottom lip as a thought occurred to her. "Are ***you*** one of those women?"

If Coral had a thing, past or present, for Xavier, it would put him squarely off limits. *Of course, she wasn't considering anything with him.* But, if her best friend had any non-platonic dealings with him, then the bestie code meant even a dalliance with Xavier was a no-go.

"Girl, please. He's fine, but besides the fact that I don't shit where I eat, I've never done more than appreciate the work it took to get his body to look the way it does.

And, he's never given me any indication he was interested in me. At all. As a matter of fact, He doesn't speak to anyone more than is strictly necessary—with the exception of his brothers that is."

"His brothers?" Esmeralda adjusted the workout tights and sat on the bench to pull on her sneakers.

"Quite a few of his MC brothers come here to workout. You met one of them the other day when I was showing you around. You don't remember Sitch?"

Esmeralda wrinkled her nose. "The guy who's spirit you crushed and ground into dust? Yes. I remember him."

Opening the door to the stall, she stepped out with her bag on her shoulder once more.

"I did ***not*** crush his spirit. Besides, Sitch isn't really into me. It just bothers him that I'm not falling all over myself because he exists in my universe."

"Sitch? Who named these people?"

Esmeralda walked down the row of lockers looking for an empty one. Similar to the occupied/vacant green and red indicators on the lavatory doors on planes, each locker was fitted with a lever which turned red when it was in use.

"Don't ask me. Who knows how MCs hand names out to prospects."

Tossing her towel over her shoulder, Esmeralda pushed her stuff into the empty locker and set the code.

"The road name thing is wild. Sitch. Toad. I wonder if there's a Road Lizard in the group."

"I wouldn't doubt it." Coral laughed as they left the locker room.

"Come on, Ezzy! Two more." Coral coaxed as Esmeralda bent her knees into a squat. She'd been a member of Sin Gym for a month and Coral was really upping the intensity of their workouts.

The weight of the bar across her shoulders felt like it was pulling her into the mat beneath her feet. Sweat dripped down her neck and she tried not to focus on its trajectory down her back into the waistband of her tights.

"Don't forget to breathe." Coral reminded her as Esmeralda straightened her legs.

"One more. You've got this."

Esmeralda loved Coral. She really did. But, when her friend was in full on trainer mode, Esmeralda wanted to cuss her. Using all the best cuss words with more than two syllables.

Powering through the last squat, Esmeralda took two steps forward with the weight on her shoulders and lowered it back onto the stand. Their reflection in the mirror showed Coral trailing behind her, arms raised to help with the load if needed.

Once Esmeralda moved away from the weights, Coral tossed her a towel and extended a water bottle. Esmeralda had forgotten her own, so Coral snagged one from the merch shop. Taking a deep draw on the refreshing drink, Esmeralda savored the cool feeling of the water gliding down her throat.

"What are you doing after this? Wanna get dinner?"

Dabbing at perspiration, Esmeralda shook her head. "Thanks, but I'm going to stop by the leather shop I saw nearby. I'm still looking for accessories for my cosplay."

"Oh yeah. I forgot you mentioned that the last time."

The two passed the free weights as they talked. While most gyms reeked of testosterone and desperation, Sin Gym seemed to have a good mix of clientele who didn't give off fitness elite vibes. So, when a few heads turned to mark their progress, Esmeralda didn't pay it any attention. Even when the eyes tracking her movements belonged to Xavier Carmichael.

Preferring to shower at home, Esmeralda said goodbye to Coral in the locker room. With her bag on her shoulder, she made her way to her vehicle. It wasn't as if she was looking for him, but she didn't see Xavier on her way out. After she became an official member, she'd seen him around, but they hadn't spoken more than a few words here or there since he left her at the door of the ladies' locker room with his impromptu nickname.

Princess Peach? Where did that come from, and why didn't she correct him? She didn't have a problem letting him know not to call her Ezzy, but she allowed him to pin a new nickname on her? She'd had time to correct him, but hadn't said a word in the past month. Shrugging off questions she didn't want to dig into, Esmeralda pulled away from the parking area and entered the flow of traffic.

It only took her five minutes to reach *Hyde and Pride Leatherworks.* She hadn't heard of the place before she drove past it to get to the gym. Finding a spot near the entrance of the storefront, she parked. Esmeralda didn't anticipate being inside long. A shower was in order after her workout, but she lived thirty minutes away. It was more convenient to stop into the store on her way home.

A man with a rugged tan complexion and a chest-length white beard was seated on a stool behind a glass display case. Rock music played in the store at a level which still allowed for conversation.

"Good evening, ma'am. Let me know if you need any help."

The man smiled transforming his face from grizzled warrior to kindly grandpa. Esmeralda couldn't stop herself from returning the gesture.

"Thank you."

She moved between the racks reading the labels on the sections. She was specifically looking for leather cuffs and similar accessories to go with her Queen Neferata costume. She was borderline obsessed with the comic book character who was loosely modeled after the Egyptian Queen, Nefertiti.

Esmeralda's eye was caught by a display of whips along one section of the wall. So, instead of perusing the cuffs in the nearby bins, she stood staring at the variety of whips, floggers and other similar items.

"Well, well, well. If it isn't Princess Peach. I never would've thought a prim little scientist like you would be into the rough stuff."

Esmeralda turned wide eyes to the owner of the deep voice sending tingles through her center. *Shit...* Xavier Carmichael.

Chapter Seven

Toad couldn't believe his luck, but he wasn't about to look a gift horse in the mouth. When the bell on the door jingled and he heard Clive call out his usual greeting, he hadn't paid much attention. He'd come to *Hyde and Pride* to get a rip repaired in the leather jacket he wore under his cut. However, when a familiar frame appeared in his peripheral vision, every part of him became fully alert.

Watching her bypass the bins of leather bracelets and accessories, his heart rate picked up when she stood before the whips, floggers and cat-o'-nine-tails. Was his little princess into bondage play? Toad wasn't a hard-core Dom, but he'd experimented. An image of Esmeralda sprawled across his bed willingly awaiting lashes turned his cock to granite.

Although she appeared mildly startled when he spoke to her, she didn't show the slightest hint of embarrassment. That was good. Very good. He wondered if she knew *Hyde and Pride* catered to the general leather enthusiast, but also to those in the BDSM lifestyle, along with bikers.

"Excuse me?"

Unable to stop himself, Toad moved closer crowding her space. "I said, I didn't think a prim little scientist like yourself was into the rough stuff. Color me surprised."

Folding her arms beneath her breast, she lifted them for his viewing pleasure. It was likely not her intent, but he enjoyed the results regardless. Her normal peachy scent was laced with the product of a vigorous workout. Instead of being a deterrent, it turned him on. Toad was certain he could come up with several ways to recreate that scent and combine it with his own.

"I have no idea what you mean."

Her lips pursed into the cutest line, and he had to shove his hands into his pockets to keep from snatching her to him and kissing the proper little expression from her face. He knew it wasn't an option. At least not now. Although she hadn't made it easy on him by remaining in the gear she'd worn to workout. The tights hugged her thick legs and generous ass perfectly. The vee neck of her tank top draped loosely, but didn't hide the bounty of her breasts. *Damn, he wanted those in his mouth.*

Forcing himself to stop thinking about shit that couldn't happen right this second, Toad flicked his gaze between her face and the various implements on the wall.

"You do realize this place caters to people in the lifestyle right?"

"Huh? Lifestyle?"

"Aww...Princess Peach, please tell me you aren't that innocent. No. Wait. It's fine if you are. I can help you shuck that innocence right off."

Esmeralda rolled her eyes at him and raised one eyebrow. "For your information, there's more than one kind of 'lifestyle'." She used air quotes around the word lifestyle. "How am I to know which one you're talking about? You could be talking about traditional Dom/Sub relationships, kinks, fetishes or something else. For all I know, you could be talking about straight up BDSM."

Listening to her rattle off the sexual and nonsexual variations of the lifestyle made him consider tugging her into the back room to discuss which of said things on her list he could tick off for her. His vote was for all of them—in whatever order she wanted to start with.

"Well, aren't you just a wealth of information?"

"If you say so." Although her voice held a slight edge, her words had no real bite. At least not one Toad cared to acknowledge.

Resting one arm along the top of the row of bins, he gestured toward the corded leather on the wall.

"Which one do you want?"

"Neither."

"Come on, Princess. You don't have to lie to me. I saw the way you were staring at the wall."

"I was simply curious."

Toad didn't miss the slight flush beneath her umber colored skin. She couldn't blame the blush on the exertion of her workout. Too much time had passed. He knew how long ago it was, because once she and Coral headed toward the locker rooms, he'd hopped on his bike and left.

Apparently, God still loved him and sent him his own personal angel to corrupt. Toad didn't bother himself with how blasphemous his thought process appeared. He was too busy trying to make the most of his current blessing.

"Like I said, Princess. You don't have to lie to me."

"I'm not lying. I came in to look for a few things, and the display caught my attention that's all."

"Mhm. Okay." Standing up straight, Toad rubbed his hands together. "What kind of things are you looking for? I might be able to help. I'm a regular customer here."

She folded her arms across her middle, once again pushing those bountiful breast up for his enjoyment. He was so enamored, he almost missed what she said.

"If you're a regular customer, I should be asking which of these things you own instead of you asking me what I want."

Toad couldn't help himself. He leaned closer to her and lowered his voice.

"Princess, everyone knows it's polite to allow your partner to choose their own toys. What would it look like for me to have a collection of items without knowing which ones you prefer?"

Esmeralda's head tipped back and her mouth dropped open slightly. Toad licked his bottom lip, and he was certain his messaging was quite clear. Before his eyes, she cycled through stages of emotions finally landing on understanding.

Tilting her pert little nose into the air, she actually sniffed at him. *So fucking cute.*

"It doesn't matter which one I'd prefer. I don't want one. Besides, I'm not one of your biker bunnies."

"Angels."

"What?"

"We call them Angels. And, I'm well aware that you aren't one of them."

Toad allowed his gaze to travel over her from head to toe, overtly projecting his attraction. It wasn't subtle. But, he wasn't exactly a subtle guy. Not when it came to something he wanted. He was amazed he'd managed to let her exist in his orbit for an entire month while doing nothing more than a little light flirting.

But, make no mistake about it, he wanted Esmeralda Upton. And he wanted her to know it. The flush beneath her beautiful brown skin intensified, and she stiffly turned her head, breaking their visual connection.

"You know what? I don't have time for this."

Facing away from the wall, she walked over to the section containing leather bracelets and cuffs. As she reached into the wire bin, he closed the distance between them. Stopping just behind her, he looked over her shoulder to see what she'd selected.

She held a black cuff style bracelet with bronzed metal at the center and leather laces on the ends. Easily lifting it from her fingers, he captured her hand and laced the cuff onto her wrist.

"You can't really know if it'll work unless you try it on."

"I was just looking at it." Esmeralda protested. She tugged her arm lightly earning a light tap from Toad.

"Stop wiggling."

"Excuse you!"

"What? I'm being helpful."

"You're being bossy and manhandling me."

Toad froze mid-action and stared at her. "I'll accept bossy, because I'm a fucking boss. But manhandling? Trust me, Princess, if I manhandle you, you will damn well be able to tell the difference. Now, be still."

He didn't miss the way her breath hitched at the command in his voice. Princess Peach liked being ordered around. He could definitely help her with that.

When he finished lacing the cuff, he reached into the bin. Grabbing an identical bracelet, he started the process on her other wrist. Once he was done, he turned her toward a nearby mirror so she could look at herself.

"What do you think? How do they feel?"

Toad stood behind Esmeralda with his hands on her shoulders. His gaze devoured her form in the mirror. Of course, the bracelets weren't meant to be worn with tights and an exercise tee, but they looked good on her arms. Images of her wearing nothing but the leather accessories flit across his mind's eye making him groan.

"They feel okay."

Lifting her arms, she turned her wrist this way and that admiringly.

"You never said why you wanted those things."

"You never asked."

Toad frowned, rewinding their conversation. Hell, she was right. He hadn't asked why she wanted them, just what she wanted. It really didn't matter why. He simply needed a way to keep the conversation going.

"Okay. So, I'm asking now. Why do you want them? Thinking of joining a MC?"

Esmeralda wrinkled her nose again. It took everything in him not to lean over and kiss it.

"What? No. It's for my cosplay."

Toad nodded. It tracked. His curvy little scientist enjoyed playing dress up. He could work with that.

"Who are you cosplaying?"

"You wouldn't know her."

Shaking her head, Esmeralda began undoing the laces to remove the bracelets. Swatting her fingers away, Toad unlaced both bracelets.

"You don't know who I know, Princess Peach. Hit me with a name. I might surprise you."

He wasn't looking directly at her, but he felt her eyes on him as he continued to remove the bracelets from her wrists. When he glanced at her, he saw the mental calculations written across her expressive face.

"I'm not making fun of you. I really wanna know."

She visibly relaxed, and he knew he'd said the right thing.

"Queen Neferata."

"From the futuristic Egyptian comic?"

Esmeralda's eyes widened in surprise. "Yes! How did you know?"

Winking, Toad tapped her wrists and held the bracelets in one hand. "I told you, Princess. I know things."

"Yes, but it's a relatively new comic. It's only been out for three years and it's not really mainstream."

"What can I say? I'm a man of mystery." Holding up the bracelets, he asked, "is there anything else you wanted, or are these it?"

"That's all I want for now. Thanks."

She reached for the bracelets and he held them up—just out of her reach.

"I've got 'em." Ignoring her pout, he hitched his thumb toward the wall. "You sure you don't want to pick out a pretty pink flogger?"

"Ugh! Stop it!"

Turning on her heel, she power walked to the register. Toad strolled behind her enjoying the view.

Chapter Eight

Esmeralda could not believe she'd not only run into Xavier at the leather shop, but had spent the past several minutes having what could be considered flirtatious banter with him. She absolutely was *not* flirting with him, but he was obviously flirting with her. Unless she was so rusty she couldn't tell the difference anymore.

A quick glance over her shoulder confirmed he was following her to where the man with the white beard sat behind the counter. His stare was firmly glued to her ass. *Of course it was.* Giving a mental eye roll, she stopped when she reached the register and waited for Xavier to catch up. With her much shorter legs, she shouldn't have outpaced him. But she may or may not have speed walked to get there first.

When he reached the glass case separating them from the older gentleman, he placed her selections on it. The other man moved the items closer and began ringing them up.

"Will there be anything else?" His gaze bounced between Esmeralda and Xavier.

"No, thank you." She murmured.

"Just add her stuff to my order, Clive."

Esmeralda's brow furrowed as she looked up at him.

"That's not necessary."

She had a hard and fast rule about allowing men to buy things for her. They tended to think everything was transactional, and she didn't have the patience for the foolishness which usually ensued.

"Don't worry about it. It's no biggie. It's not like you took me up on my other offer."

His statement zapped all the fight from her. Heat crept up Esmeralda's neck and she knew she had added color in her cheeks. Whoever started the myth about black people not visibly blushing had obviously never met anyone like her. The way her face burned, she knew it showed. She couldn't believe he'd brought up the whip conversation in front of a stranger.

Okay, so he didn't actually overtly say it, but he'd alluded to it. That was enough by itself. *This man was a menace*. Esmeralda was certain he knew it too.

She didn't respond to his taunt. Instead, she accepted the small plastic bag and quietly offered her thanks. Internally, she heard her cousin's voice urging her to loosen up. To let a man do something for her sometime.

"Give me a minute, Toad. I'll check to see how much longer it'll be."

"Take your time, Clive. I'm gonna see the little lady to her car and I'll be back."

Esmeralda bristled at being called a little lady. It reeked of misogyny. But what did she expect from a biker? As soon as the thought floated into her mind, she regretted even thinking it. It was extremely judgmental and not at all like her.

She had no idea why Xavier Carmichael rubbed her the wrong way. The tiny voice, she ignored on most days, piped up to suggest it was because there were other ways she wanted him to rub her, but Esmeralda muzzled the horny little instigator. She was *so* not going there.

The weight of Xavier's hand pressed against the small of her back and despite her big talk, she allowed him to guide her from the store. She'd managed to snag a parking space almost directly in front. However, she didn't immediately see her SUV because of the big white van parked alongside it.

It was only when she was right up on it that she realized it was leaning awkwardly. Slowing to a stop, her head dropped and a few choice curse words flew from her mouth.

"Whoa, Princess. Is that the mouth you wanna kiss me with?"

Ignoring Xavier's teasing, she pointed at her tires. "Two of my tires are flat. Damnit!!"

Thinking to get a closer look, she went to step off the curb. A strong arm barred her from moving forward.

"Hold up. Let me check it out. You stay right here where I can see you."

Frowning, she stared at him. "What? I'm perfectly capable of looking at a flat tire."

Xavier pierced her with those dark eyes. The expression on his face was a far cry from the playful one he'd worn mere seconds earlier.

"I'm serious, Esmeralda. Stay right there and let me look at it."

Freezing on the sidewalk, Esmeralda did as she was told. Him using her real name instead of the one he'd tagged her with spoke of his seriousness about the situation.

Reaching into the pocket on the side of her tights, she pulled her cellphone free.

"Fine. I'll call for Roadside Service. Maybe they have someone close who can tow it to a garage. I only have one spare. So, I won't be driving away regardless."

As she talked, Xavier walked a circle around her vehicle. At each tire, he stooped and examined it closely. She watched with open curiosity as the phone rang in her ear. He'd completed his inspection before someone finally answered the phone.

"Hi, I was calling about a tow. I have two flat tires."

"Three." Xavier corrected while plucking the phone from her fingers. "Cancel that order." He barked into the phone before pressing the icon to end the call.

"Excuse you! What is your deal?" Esmeralda couldn't believe his high-handed behavior.

Xavier's body was rigid as his eyes swept the parking lot and the area surrounding the storefront. His focus was so intense, she forgot her protest and started looking around as well.

"What is it?" After what seemed like forever without him saying anything, she finally asked.

Instead of answering, he guided her back inside the leather goods store. Once the door closed behind them, she twisted to face him again.

"What is it? You're starting to creep me out."

"Do you have any enemies?"

Esmeralda's head rocked back on her neck. "Enemies? Not that I know of. Why?"

"Your flat tires aren't a coincidence. They were deliberately cut."

"Are you serious?" Without thought, she moved toward the door to go see for herself.

"What are you doing? Get back here." Xavier stopped her before she even reached the handle.

"I wanna see."

"Well, I want you safe. So, you're staying your ass right here until I figure something out." Xavier's voice had a hard, commanding edge.

Esmeralda's heart raced. She didn't know if it was from hearing someone deliberately vandalized her vehicle or due to her standoff with Xavier. Not knowing what was going on didn't sit right with her, and being denied the opportunity to see it with her own eyes wasn't going to fly.

Why did he think it was his job to keep her safe? They'd met for the first time barely a month ago. He didn't know her from a hole in the wall. Not really. His bodyguard routine didn't mesh with what she'd learned about him.

While she debated how to handle the situation, the older man working the register approached them with a leather jacket in his hands.

"Here ya go, Toad. We got it all fixed up for you."

"Thanks, Clive." Xavier took the jacket, but didn't put it on. Clive started to walk away when Xavier called out to him. "Hey, Clive. Do those cameras outside work or are they for show?"

"They work. A few of the businesses down the strip from us had a problem with break-ins a couple of years back. After that, we added two more to monitor the area around the entrance and not just the front door."

"Do you think I can have a look?"

To Esmeralda's surprise, Clive didn't bat an eye at the request.

"Sure. Come to the office."

Yielding to Xavier's guiding hand on her back, Esmeralda followed Clive. They moved through the racks to reach the office and Clive asked the question she felt he should've asked before agreeing to let them see the footage.

"Did something happen outside?"

"That's what I want to see." Xavier's expression remained hard and determined.

Clive led them into the small office. They entered, and he rounded the desk to press a button on the keyboard waking the monitors. Sitting behind the desk, Clive made a few mouse clicks to bring up a sliding bar along the bottom of the screen.

Keeping her at his side, Xavier placed one hand on the desktop as he leaned in to see the images.

"Go back about thirty minutes." Xavier instructed.

Esmeralda found it curious since they were inside the store for a maximum of twenty minutes—including the time it took to check out. Her naturally curious nature was amplified by being at the center of a situation with no answers.

There was no sound with the video, so they watched silently as cars came and went and a few people walked past the front of the store. Esmeralda saw when Xavier entered the parking lot. The video showed him opening the storage compartment beneath his seat and placing his cut inside.

Almost ten minutes after he walked into the store, she saw herself. The space to her immediate left was empty when she arrived, but there was a car in the next available space. Which was probably why she didn't notice the big black Harley Davidson motorcycle Xavier rode up on.

She was only inside for a few minutes when the white van pulled into the space next to her vehicle. The person driving didn't exit, but disappeared into the darkness of the interior of the van. There was no other movement until she and Xavier exited the store.

They never saw anyone approach her vehicle the entire time. Esmeralda's brow furrowed as she watched the playback of herself and Xavier on the sidewalk.

"That doesn't make any sense." She nibbled her lip as she stared at the screen.

"It makes perfect fucking sense to me." Xavier growled. He stood to his full height and stalked to the door.

"Stay here with Clive."

The directive was tossed over his shoulder as he cut a quick path through the shop. He was through the front door before the bell dinged in her head to put the pieces together. Whoever was in the white van cut her tires. The sliding door of the van wasn't in view of the camera. It would've been easy for someone to exit without being seen. They were probably waiting for her to come out alone. If Xavier hadn't been with her, she could've been kidnapped.

The reality of the situation hit her like a sledge hammer and her knees buckled.

"Whoa there, pretty lady." Clive exclaimed. He barely moved in time to help lower her into the only other chair in the small office.

Chapter Nine

Even as he raced to the front of the store, Toad knew the van wouldn't be there. When he crashed through the front entrance, the space next to Esmeralda's vehicle was empty. Cursing, he stepped off the sidewalk and walked out into the parking lot to try to see the road in the distance. Nothing either way.

"Fuck!"

Those motherfuckers had been lying in wait for Esmeralda. He didn't even wanna think about what would've happened if he hadn't insisted on walking her to her car. Patting his pockets, he searched for his cellphone. When he felt one in either of his back pockets, he frowned. *Shit*. He still had her phone.

Sliding it back into his jeans, he unlocked his phone and made a call. It connected on the second ring. Not giving the man on the other end a chance to do more than say hello, Toad launched into his orders.

"Fubar, grab a few prospects and meet me at the clubhouse."

"I'm already here."

"Good. Round up the prospects and be ready when I get there."

Not bothering to say goodbye, Toad ended the call and strode back into the store. The door to the office was wide open allowing him to see inside. When he noticed Clive leaning over Esmeralda, he picked up the pace.

Not slowing down until he was standing beside her, Toad stooped to look into her face.

"Hey there, Princess. You okay?"

"No. I'm not okay. I was almost kidnapped. What part of your mind would make you ask me if I'm okay?"

Considering the situation, Toad could accept a little snap back this one time. She had some real shit dumped on her at once. Anyone with half a brain cell and valued their safety would be at least a little rattled. If she wasn't shaken at all, he'd be suspicious. Clive was still hovering. Toad shot him a glance. Holding his hands up, Clive backed away.

While he knew he should be grateful the older man was there to help Esmeralda when she needed it, Toad didn't like how invested he seemed. He also didn't like thinking he wasn't the only man experiencing an immediate draw to her. Whether she was aware or not, she was magnetic.

"Come on, Princess. I'm gonna take you somewhere safe."

Esmeralda accepted his help standing from the chair, but he read the set of her jaw. She wouldn't simply fall in line with his plan.

"Can I have my phone please?"

The question was posed with such polite calmness, it immediately put Toad on high alert. He passed her the phone without comment as they left Clive's little office.

"Thanks, Clive."

Toad knew his words and tone clashed, but his mama had taught him *some* manners. The old man had proven helpful. Watching Esmeralda, their height difference made it easy for him to look over her shoulder to see what she was doing on her phone. They'd just reached the exit when the bubble for a rideshare app appeared on the screen. Without missing a step, he plucked the device from her fingers again.

"Will you stop doing that?!"

Esmeralda whirled on him. This time she didn't bother to try grabbing at it. If looks could kill, his mama would have somewhere to wear her black dress she reserved for only one occasion.

"Princess, you were almost a victim of something pretty fucked up. I'm not about to let you get into a car with a stranger."

"***Let me***?"

Her expression hid nothing of how she felt about his choice of words. Toad wouldn't take it back though. He meant it. He wasn't letting her get her little ass in a stranger's car. She was leaving, but only on the back of his bike.

"Yeah, Princess. I'm not *letting* you drive off with some stranger. We don't know if whoever drove the van is lying in wait on your route home or not. So, for the time being, you're going with me."

If her folded arms weren't a hint, the tapping of her foot was a clear indicator. She was about to blow. Toad let her stew on her thoughts while he walked to his bike. Opening the top box, he pulled out a spare helmet along with his cut. Transferring both of their phones to the storage area, he closed it.

Slipping the cut over his shoulders, he turned to see her exactly where he left her. Instead of approaching her, he leaned against his bike and crossed his legs at the ankle. He checked his watch, but he wasn't in any rush. The clubhouse was roughly a fifteen-minute ride.

Fubar might need the extra time to find the prospects he knew Toad would want. Every man isn't built for every job. Being an enforcer could get sticky quickly. Having his brother from the mother chapter in Las Vegas relocate to Oakland had come in handy.

Toad watched as Esmeralda conducted her internal debate. Her face was so expressive, he could tell part of the discussion involved her trying to kick his ass and take her stuff back. When she finally made eye contact with him, he simply cocked an eyebrow and tilted his head. Obeying the unspoken demand, she slowly walked toward him.

He wasn't in the Dom/Sub lifestyle, but Esmeralda showed brat tendencies. Damn if she didn't bring out the urge within him to investigate it simply for the pleasure of taming her. When she was within reach, he tugged her closer. Not crowding her, but not enough space between them for another person to wedge themselves.

This time, when she spoke, her voice lacked the confrontational edge. "Why are you doing this? You don't even know me."

"I know enough."

Picking up the jacket he'd laid across the seat, he held it up to her.

"Here. You'll need to put this on. It's warm out, but I can't have you on my bike without something covering your arms."

Esmeralda took a small step back. The cute little crinkle of her nose reappeared. "You expect me to ride on that thing with you?"

"That's the plan. My truck is parked at a garage not too far from here. We can switch over, but we have to get there first."

He didn't feel it was necessary to mention the garage was next to the clubhouse on the compound. It was irrelevant. They weren't going inside, anyway. No matter that he'd already claimed her in his own mind, neither of them were ready for such a step. It was definitely too much too fast. Her big brain might go into overload at the implication.

"This jacket is too big and too little at the same time. I can't wear this."

Toad ignored Esmeralda's complaint and adjusted the sleeves. They hung well past her hands. Once he was done, at least her fingertips were visible. She was right in that it wouldn't zip all the way up. Those distracting breasts of hers made it a no go. Getting the bottom snapped was going to have to be enough.

"There." He tugged at the lapels keeping her in place between his outstretched legs. "It's fine for the length of time you'll need it."

Thankfully, she'd tamed her coily hair into a low ponytail, so the helmet fit without issue. Although she let him put it on her, she still looked hesitant. Releasing a huffing breath, he rested his hands on her shoulders.

"Spit it out, Princess."

"This is all ***a lot*** to process at one time. I have no idea why you're so invested, and I don't know why anyone would try to kidnap me. None of this makes sense. And, I've never been on a motorcycle. I'm not sure I want today to be the first time. Not when I'm feeling so out of sorts. Maybe we should go back to the original plan. I'll call for a tow. I can concede the rideshare wasn't my finest idea. So, I can call Coral. She lives closer than I do. She could be here in less than an hour."

Toad let her ramble without interruption. He seemed to innately know she needed to get it all out. His prompting had her spilling her internal processing out into the open. When she started in on calling someone else to help her, he shook his head. That shit wasn't going to happen. Hell, he'd just decided she wasn't leaving his sight until he knew what the fuck was going on.

He shifted her backwards until he had enough room to stand up straight. Holding onto one of her hands, he threw his leg over the motorcycle he'd lovingly named Charmaine. He released her hand only long enough to put on his helmet and raise the kick stand. He held off on pressing the ignition switch.

"Get on."

Part of Esmeralda's bottom lip disappeared between her teeth as she looked at Charmaine skeptically. Tugging her forward, he cupped the side of her face. Maintaining eye contact, he stroked her cheek.

"It's gonna be fine. I'll keep you safe."

Pressing a quick kiss to her forehead, he nudged her to use the rear footrest to climb onto the bike behind him. Once she was seated, he grasped each of her hands in turn and placed them on his waist. She didn't have a good grip, so he tapped her fingers.

"Hold on tight." Appealing to her scientific side, he explained the dynamics of being able to control the machine. He even dipped into the physics a little.

"It's easier for us to maintain balance if we move like one unit. We can't do that if you're as far away as you can get and barely hanging on."

Toad almost groaned aloud when Esmeralda's soft bosom pressed into his back and her plush thighs rested at his hips. The fifteen-minute ride to the clubhouse was going to take for-fucking-ever.

Chapter Ten

Esmeralda held on to Xavier tightly. At that point he was her literal lifeline. He didn't do anything daring or unsafe. And, he kept the motorcycle at a speed which didn't have her clenching her butt cheeks so hard she could form diamonds.

Although, a couple of turns had her rethinking her assessment. During those times, he patted her hand in reassurance, but he kept going. It was nice to know he had a softer side contrasting the dominant hard-ass he turned into right before her eyes.

Initially, she closed her eyes to try to block out how quickly the world was passing by without the security of a car's metal cage surrounding her. However, loss of vision heightened her other senses. Toad's hard body should've been uncomfortable, but he felt amazing in every place they were pressed together.

The scent of the leather filled her nose, but it didn't disguise the masculine smell of his cologne. She couldn't pinpoint the fragrance, but the combination of the aroma with the way his muscles felt against her softness had her popping her eyes open. Esmeralda would take the potential fear over tumbling down a horny rabbit hole.

When they left the highway and turned onto a road with fewer structures lining the street, she became more alert. Had she made a mistake coming with him? Should she have demanded her phone and called Coral to come and get her? When a collection of buildings came into view, she strained her eyes trying to read any available signage.

Was that...? The same skull wearing a crown, which graced the back of Xavier's cut, was prominently displayed on the side of one building. Seeing the image caused her to stiffen as tension tightened every muscle.

He'd brought her to the Sin City compound. *What the hell was he thinking?* She should ***not*** be here. Esmeralda's fingers clenched around the leather of Xavier's cut. His large, warm hand covered one of hers delivering a light pat as if he knew she needed the extra assurance. While it felt good, it did absolutely nothing to calm her.

Xavier slowly steered the bike into a space near the front entrance of what could only be the clubhouse. The sign above it designated the space for the Sergeant at Arms. Esmeralda hadn't paid much attention to the different patches on his cut at the store. However, when he swung off of the bike and extended his hand to her, she raked her eyes over each one.

On one side 'Toad' was stitched intricately. Directly beneath it was a patch bearing the title SGT AT ARMS. *How the hell had she missed that?*

She still didn't understand why a man so handsome let anyone call him by such an unattractive moniker. However, what she knew about the biker life was just enough to keep her from committing any major faux pas. Esmeralda wouldn't say she was well versed at all.

Xavier tugged her to follow him, but her feet refused to move. There was no way she was going inside the clubhouse. She knew enough to understand exactly what it meant. No matter what the circumstances surrounding why she was there, that was a hard and fast rule.

When she didn't move, he turned to look at her. Those dark eyes probed her. Esmeralda felt like he was looking directly into her soul. She wasn't sure she liked it. At all.

"What's wrong? We'll only be here a few minutes. I need to grab a few things."

"I'll wait here."

Her reply was met with vigorous head shaking. "Absolutely not. You're not hanging around out here alone. Besides, visitors require an escort at all times. Club rules."

Chewing on her bottom lip, she stared between him and the front of the building. There was no way she was going inside that club. Esmeralda's heart began to race. She didn't think Xavier would hurt her, but she couldn't say for certain. This was the most time they'd spent in one another's presence since she signed up at the gym.

Xavier's cheeks puffed out slightly as he exhaled deeply. Stepping into her space, he cupped the side of her face with one hand.

"Princess, I promise. You're safe with me."

"I'm not dumb, Xavier. I may not know everything about club life, but I know what walking inside that building with you means."

His eyes widened for a split second. He shook his head before placing a kiss on her brow.

"You let me worry about the implications. Just stay close."

"I'll wait here."

"Esmeralda, we don't have time for this."

She didn't know when it happened, but she'd started to dislike him calling her by her given name. Even though she'd baulked internally at being called Princess Peach, when he'd first said it. Her jaw stiffened under his touch and she stared at him mutinously. She was serious about staying right where she was.

A motorcycle rolled into the space next to the one they occupied and Xavier looked slightly relieved to see the biker who pulled off his helmet. Esmeralda did a quick double-take. The other guy looked enough like Xavier for her to wonder if they were blood brothers and not simply MC brothers.

"Hey, Frenchie. I need a favor."

Frenchie stowed his helmet and stood next to his bike. His response was a simple raised eyebrow. Apparently, it was enough for Xavier because he began talking.

"I need to run inside. Can you keep the princess company for a few minutes?"

Without conscious thought, Esmeralda's fingers gripped the t-shirt Xavier wore underneath his cut. She didn't even realize she'd been touching him until that moment.

She watched as the two held a silent conversation resulting in Frenchie giving Xavier what passed for a nod and folding his arms over his chest.

"Princess, Frenchie is going to stay with you while I go inside. I won't be long."

Esmeralda tried to maintain her grip as Xavier pried her fingers from his shirt. She didn't want to go inside with him, but she didn't like the idea of him leaving her with someone she didn't know.

"This is Frenchie. He's our chaplain. I trust him. He'll look out for you. I promise, I won't be long."

"You go on inside brother. I won't let anything happen to the lady."

Esmeralda looked at Frenchie. He offered her a polite nod and a head tilt. It made him seem less intimidating. She still wouldn't test him, but she didn't get bad vibes from him.

Squeezing her fingers, Toad maneuvered her closer to his bike. Giving Frenchie a parting nod, his long legs ate up the pavement. He disappeared behind the heavy doors of the clubhouse.

When Esmeralda looked back at Frenchie, his eyes were scanning the lot. His muscular arms were crossed over his chest as he leaned against his bike. Unlike Xavier, he rode an Indian instead of a Harley.

Not really sure what to do with herself, Esmeralda leaned a hip against Xavier's bike and looked around. It might not have been what she should've done, but she was curious by nature. The front doors opened and her heart lifted.

Her shoulders dropped as her hope of it being Xavier was dashed. A guy too handsome for his own good walked out with another, larger guy trailing behind him. Hot on their heels was a leggy brunette wearing a barely-there bralette top and a mini skirt.

"Fubar, where are you and Trick off to so fast? I thought we were gonna have some fun?"

The pretty biker didn't even look at the brunette when he replied. "Can't play with you now, Lacey. I promised Trick I'd braid his hair. You know how he gets when his hair's not perfect."

Trick didn't say a word to refute Fubar's statement and Esmeralda stifled a laugh. How desperate was that chick? She was throwing her pussy at a man who obviously didn't want her. Trick separated from the two, but Fubar continued walking in their direction. Lacey was still trying to hang on though. It was actually kind of sad.

"Come on Fubar...You know I'll do that thing you like. I'll do ***all*** the things you like."

"Can't. After I braid Trick's hair, I'm giving Frenchie a mani-pedi."

Esmeralda couldn't contain her laughter at his reply. By then, the two were standing less than ten feet away from her. The brunette's steps faltered as Esmeralda's laughter drew her attention.

This close, even with the make-up and poor wardrobe decisions, Esmeralda recognized Deena Hall. Obviously, Deena recognized her as well, because she immediately stopped begging Fubar and started back pedaling.

"That's okay, Fubar. I know when I'm not wanted. There are other brothers who'd be happy to have my mouth on them."

"Tell them to keep the penicillin handy."

Esmeralda probably would have laughed had she not been so shocked to see an FBI agent walking back inside the Sin City MC clubhouse. Not just an FBI agent, but one who normally did undercover work involving human trafficking. If she was here, did it mean the club was in the flesh trade in more ways than one?

She wasn't under the delusion the Oakland Chapter would veer too far from the Las Vegas Chapter. Born and raised in Las Vegas, she'd heard more than a few things about the Sinners and their activities. A person would have to live under a rock not to hear about the Sin City MC.

So, she wouldn't be surprised to learn not all of their dealings were legal. However, she had never heard of them to be a part of the flesh peddling game.

Her skin heated and her heart pulsed for an entirely different reason than before. Two more men exited before Xavier re-appeared. His gaze swept the lot as bikes roared to life. Stopping in front of her, he stared at her assessingly.

"What's wrong, Princess?"

Chapter Eleven

Toad couldn't explain how he knew, but he was aware that all wasn't right with Esmeralda the moment he stepped out of the clubhouse. She'd been uncomfortable when he left, but she looked petrified when he returned.

He knew it wasn't anything Frenchie had done. His brother might look fierce, but he wouldn't hurt her. Hell, he probably hadn't spoken a word to her the entire time. Toad searched the parking area for what or who could've spooked her so thoroughly. She looked as shaken as when she learned she'd barely escaped kidnapping.

Leaning down to get closer to her face, he asked again, "Princess, what's wrong?"

Uncertainty mixed with the fear in her expression. Indecision he could deal with, but the idea of her being afraid made him feral. *What the fuck happened?*

He looked at Frenchie with questions in his eyes. Frenchie simply shrugged. Frenchie didn't know what was up with her either. They'd been friends so long sometimes actual words weren't needed. Which was fine, since Frenchie wasn't a fan of unnecessary talking.

Tugging Esmeralda's hand, he pulled her toward the four-level structure next to the clubhouse. He and some of the other brothers kept their alternative vehicles in the club's parking garage. Thankfully, she didn't put on the same show as when he tried to take her into the clubhouse.

It wasn't his smartest move. He wanted her, but he knew more than that was required to take her inside. Toad couldn't explain what made him change his original plan other than he'd forgotten he'd need to go inside before changing over to his truck. Making her his old lady would've been the only option for them if she'd set one toe inside the building, because he was damn sure not sharing her with anyone else. She might look angelic, but she was no Angel.

Reaching his dual-cab pickup, he opened the passenger door and helped Esmeralda inside. She still hadn't said a word to him, but she got into the vehicle with a little less reluctance than she climbed on his bike. When he was seated behind the wheel, he turned to her again.

"Tell me what's wrong, Princess. It's just the two of us now. No one can hear."

Nibbling on her bottom lip, she stared out of the front window for a few seconds before she looked at him. Questions simmered behind her soulful brown eyes and creased the area between her brows.

"Are you guys like the Sin City MC in Las Vegas?"

It wasn't the question he expected, but it was one Toad could answer.

"That's our mother chapter. So, yes. We adhere to those same bylaws."

"So, you guys are one percenters?"

Toad's brow furrowed as he tried to understand why she was suddenly on this track.

"Princess, where is this coming from? If you know about Sin City, then you know I can't discuss club business."

Esmeralda turned her gaze to the view outside the passenger side window. She was once again giving her bottom lip hell. Grasping her chin, Toad turned her face back to his.

"I don't know if it's what happened at Clive's or something else, but you're safe with me. I won't let anything happen to you."

Knowing he could come off as intense, Toad tried to project the confidence she seemed to need in order to trust him. After a short stare down, he realized he wasn't going to get her to talk. Not yet. She needed time.

"I'm going to have your car towed to a garage we use. I'll need your key. Then, I'll take you home."

Holding out his hand, he waited. Her expression was still wary as she dug into the pocket along the leg of her tights and pulled out her keys. Taking the vehicle fob off the ring, she dropped it into his hand.

Tucking it into his pocket, he started the truck. As they reached the exit of the parking structure, a tow truck fell in behind them. Trick always kept one of his trucks in the clubhouse lot, just in case someone needed a tow.

When they drove past the clubhouse, Fubar and a few of the prospects got into formation with them—two in front of Toad and two behind Trick. Fubar already knew where they were going first. Ordinarily, a road trip would involve Nitro. But Esmeralda didn't live in another club's territory. So, Toad didn't feel the need to bother the road captain.

Toad knew at some point he'd have to loop King into the whole deal. But, he wanted to get more information first. It was one thing to grab a few prospects and their newest club transplant. It was entirely different if he wanted things to go further than fixing tires and taking a lady home.

The drive back to *Hyde and Pride* was shorter since he didn't have to worry about his speed. He'd ridden slower to keep from making Esmeralda any more anxious than necessary. Though, for her first time on a bike, she did well.

When they arrived at the store, Fubar took a prospect inside the with him. They were going to look at the video footage for themselves and get the copy Toad failed to ask Clive for the first time around. The other two prospects helped him and Trick get Esmeralda's SUV loaded onto the tow truck.

Other than when she got out to remove necessary items from her vehicle, Esmeralda sat in Toad's truck. He was surprised she'd done as he asked without a fight, but he figured the shock of the situation was settling in on her. Just as Trick drove away, Fubar and his shadow exited the shop.

Waving his phone at Toad, he let him know the copy of the video was secured. Giving him a fist bump, Toad climbed into his vehicle. Esmeralda was tapping away at her cellphone screen.

"Put your address in the GPS, baby. I'll take you home."

Esmeralda looked up from the screen as if she hadn't noticed his return.

"Huh?"

"Put your address in the GPS."

Looking around at Fubar and the guys idling behind them in the parking lot, she turned a questioning gaze onto Toad.

"Are those guys going to follow us again?"

"Yes."

"Is that necessary?"

"It's a precaution. Like I said, we don't know who was driving the van, if they know where you live, or if they're lurking about looking for another opportunity.

We don't even know what they want. It could be run of the mill human trafficking or something else."

Thinking of the possibilities was what was going to keep Toad on edge until he knew. He'd ignored the question conveyed in Frenchie's expression at the clubhouse. Toad had only talked to him about her once. Then, he shows up with the woman on the back of his bike.

He was invested in her and he didn't plan on letting anyone fuck with her. Not as long as he was around. Giving her a hard look, he matched the stubborn set of her jaw. Instead of asking her to put in the address again, he put it in himself.

Toad had an amazing memory. His parents didn't understand why he wasn't interested in doing more with his college degree than running a gym. They thought it was a waste of his brain power. Don't even talk about his association with a biker gang—as they called it.

"If you knew it, why did you ask me?"

Ignoring her snippy tone, Toad gave her spandex covered thigh a few pats before resting his hand there. Amazingly, she didn't push it away. A smile crept onto his face. *He was getting to her.*

"I didn't want to be rude."

"Why start being polite now?"

A chuckle rumbled in Toad's chest. It seemed the fight hadn't completely left his little spitfire princess. Not bothering to respond, he sent the address to Fubar so that the Enforcer could lead the way.

After thirty minutes, they entered a very nice gated community. So nice it made Toad wonder just how much it paid to be a Forensic Odontologist. He wouldn't know since Esmeralda was the first person he'd met in the field. Regular dentists, he had an idea about, but she wasn't just any dentist.

Chapter Twelve

Esmeralda couldn't believe she'd led not one, not two, but five outlaw bikers into her nice quiet neighborhood. She could already see the emails from the HOA about noise ordinances. They wouldn't come out and say unsavory characters for fear of being sued, but she'd know what they meant.

Their small entourage of motorcycles and a pickup truck being escorted like she was some famous dignitary was bound to get attention. The two lead bikes pulled into her driveway. Using the app on her phone, she opened the door remotely. She never used the spare garage door openers. They lived in the junk drawer in her kitchen.

During the entire ride from the compound Esmeralda warred with herself about what she should do surrounding what she knew about the woman the Sinners called Lacey but she knew as Deena Hall. She wanted to talk to Coral about it, but Xavier had been stuck to her like glue. Even when he was helping to load her car onto the tow truck, he was constantly checking in on her.

Esmeralda texted her friend, but she didn't go into detail about Deena. She started with filling her in on her situation. Had she not started the first text with the words 'Please don't call me', she knew Coral would've immediately called once she told her about the cut tires and possible kidnapping attempt.

Coral's reassurance that Xavier would look out for her helped ease a portion of Esmeralda's anxiety, but it didn't take it away completely. There was still the matter of Deena Hall and what she was doing there.

Esmeralda had an opportunity to work with the feds on an identification case and Deena was one of the agents. Not the agent in charge. Esmeralda probably wouldn't have even remembered her if she hadn't tried to manipulate results to make it appear that additional bodies found were associated with the same case.

Thankfully, it was caught before the trial, but Deena almost tanked the whole case. Esmeralda was surprised the agent wasn't fired. However, she'd heard rumors of Deena being related to someone with power within the organization. If that was true, she'd have to do more than put her thumb on the scale to get the boot.

Based on past experiences, Esmeralda didn't respect or like the woman. She was dirty. But her being there meant there was a possibility there were lives in danger. Women and children who'd been taken against their will. On the other hand, if Deena was up to her old dirty tricks and the Sinners weren't involved in human trafficking, then Esmeralda would feel terrible for letting them continue to deal with her unknowingly. Deena only cared about winning and advancing her case—no matter who got hurt.

The conundrum gave Esmeralda a stomach ache. So far, Xavier and his brothers had done nothing but be kind and protective of her. It couldn't all be because he wanted to have sex with her. A man who looked like him didn't have to go to such lengths to get laid.

His actions were an indicator the 'bad boy' wasn't as bad as his outward appearance might have people believe. Once the garage door was up, Xavier drove his truck all the way inside. Not stopping until he was within inches of the back wall. Then, he cut the engine.

"Um...Thank you for bringing me home." Esmeralda stared at him with wide eyes. His intentions finally dawned on her. He planned to come inside.

"You don't have to stay. I have a great security system." Waving her phone at him, she pressed a button to disarm the alarm.

"Yeah...showing me that thing isn't going to cut it, Princess. I need to come inside and check things out. Fubar and the guys will walk around outside and check the perimeter."

"That's really not necessary—"

Anything else Esmeralda would've said died in her throat as Xavier hopped out of the cab and closed the door. Seconds later, he was at the passenger side with her gym bag on his shoulder and his hand extended to help her out.

Ignoring how good his roughened palm felt against hers, she climbed down from the high vehicle. The ball of anxiety in her abdomen was in conflict with the effects his touch had on her neglected core. Never one to be led by her libido, Esmeralda was at a loss as to what to do. She *really* needed to talk to Coral.

The door from the garage opened into a small mudroom before leading into the kitchen. Habit made Esmeralda slip off her sneakers and slide her feet into the fuzzy house shoes she loved. From her peripheral, she noticed Xavier unlacing and removing his boots.

She hadn't asked him to, but she appreciated the courtesy. Esmeralda did wonder how extensive his review of her system would be with him traipsing around in his sock feet.

"Where do you want me to put this?"

Xavier held up her bag of belongings. Esmeralda reached out to take it from him.

"You can give it to me. I need to go through it before I put it away."

There was a brief tug of war as if he didn't want to let her have it, then he released it. Esmeralda walked into the kitchen and placed the bag on a chair. Spinning to face him, she folded her arms.

"Okay. Now what?"

Xavier stepped into her space forcing her to tip her head back to maintain eye contact.

"Now, you take me around so I can make sure this place is secure."

Esmeralda's internal war raged almost violently. She wondered if he could tell and was simply not mentioning it. Was she really going to allow him to assess security vulnerabilities when she wasn't even sure if he and his MC could be trusted? Wouldn't that be like the rabbit letting the wolf inside and presenting all the other bunnies for slaughter?

Her phone buzzed giving her an excuse to move away from Xavier and his confusing presence.

"Hello?"

"Hey girl, now tell me what's going on. I read your texts, but I'm having a hard time wrapping my mind around it all. Not to mention you were pretty cagey about what the other thing was you needed to talk to me about."

As she listened to Coral, Esmeralda's gaze was on Xavier. He stood larger than life in her eat-in kitchen. His fingers were hooked into the loops of his jeans and his head was tilted to the side. A questioning scowl caused a dip between his eyebrows.

Pointing to the phone, she started backing out of the room. "I'm sorry. I need to take this."

Asking Coral to give her a second, she walked as fast as her legs would carry her to her bedroom. Closing and locking the door behind her she continued on to the closet in her bathroom securing all the doors along the way. Once she was safely ensconced in her walk-in closet, she leaned against the butler cabinet and put her head in her hands.

"Coral, I don't know what is going on and my stomach is in knots right now."

"Ezzy, it's understandable for you to be upset. It's possible you were almost kidnapped."

"It's not that. Well. Not *all* that. I'll process it later. This is about what I saw when Xavier took me with him to the clubhouse."

"Wait. Back up. You didn't say anything about going to the clubhouse. What the hell were you thinking? The only women allowed at an MCs clubhouse are club whores and old ladies. We both know you are neither. Unless there's something else you wanna tell me."

"Trust me. If it were up to me, I would've called roadside service, had my car towed and taken a rideshare home. Xavier wouldn't have it."

"Oh."

"Yeah. Oh. And to top it off. While I was there, I saw someone I'm certain I wasn't supposed to see."

"Who?"

Esmeralda stood and began pacing in a circle around the space. "Do you remember a couple of years ago when I was working with the FBI on identifying the remains of several young women and girls?"

"Yeah... That was so messed up."

"I know. Well, I saw the undercover agent who almost tanked the whole case. But she was dressed like a sex worker and throwing her pussy at one of the club members."

"What?! If I'm remembering the right case, it involved human trafficking."

"You're remembering correctly."

"Why the hell was an undercover FBI agent at the Sin City clubhouse?"

"That's what I want to know."

"Did you tell Toad?"

"No! Why do you think my stomach is in knots? If I tell him, who knows what they'll do to her. She's FBI, and she infiltrated a group of one percenters."

"You have to tell Toad. Sin City isn't like the outlaw bikers you heard about. I don't know what they're into, but I'm positive it's not selling people—for any reason."

A noise made Esmeralda freeze. Shushing Coral, she listened intently for a few seconds. Hearing nothing else, she returned to the call.

"How are you so sure they aren't into the kind of stuff that would get the FBI's attention? You work at the Sin Gym. You don't hang out with them outside of work. Right?"

"Listen, Ezzy. Do you trust me?"

"Of course. You're my best friend."

"And I've never lied to you. I won't start now. If it's one thing I know, it's that your FBI friend is barking up the wrong tree. They don't fuck with little kids and the only women they deal with are consenting adults. You need to tell Toad about her. It'll be bad if he finds out on his own. Don't let the smart-ass attitude fool you. He's scary observant."

Esmeralda's response lodged in her throat turning into a startled squeak as the closet door swung open and she found herself face to face with a not very happy-looking Xavier Carmichael.

Chapter Thirteen

Toad knew something was up the moment she backed away from him and exited the kitchen. No. Scratch that. Something had been off since before they left the clubhouse. Esmeralda was spooked—and it wasn't the failed kidnapping attempt.

He considered giving her space; then he heard a door close in the distance. The sound set off alarm bells. What did she have to say that was so private she needed to go into another room and close the door? Slowly, he followed the direction of the sound.

The doors to the right of the living room were open, so he walked through the room to the hallway on the opposite side. Of the two doors off the corridor, only one was closed. Without hesitation, he approached it. A quick test and his suspicions were confirmed. It was locked.

It only took a minute to go back to his truck to get his lock picks. In no time he was standing on the other side of the previously locked door. Standard locks on interior doors were child's play. Toad didn't waste time perusing the interior of her bedroom. He stalked toward the next closed door, then the next—performing the same routine until he laid eyes on Esmeralda again.

She was standing in the rear of a walk-in closet clutching the phone to her ear. Faintly, he heard the person on the other end speaking to her. His gaze raked over her from head to toe before he erased the space between them. Plucking the phone from her limp digits, he put it to his ear.

"Hey, Coral. We'll call you back later. Princess and I need to have a talk."

"Toad, you're my boss and we've always been cool. But—"

Toad interrupted what he knew was coming. "No need for threats. The princess and I just need to have a little chat. She'll call you later."

Unlike the last time he confiscated her phone, Esmeralda looked anywhere but at him. There was no indignant complaint. She didn't even question how he came to be inside her locked closet. No. No words were spoken as she pressed her palms to her stomach like she was trying to hold her insides together. It was obvious to him that whatever she was hiding away talking to Coral about had her all twisted up inside.

Sliding her phone into his pocket, he ran his fingertips down her arms. Goosebumps followed the path of his digits and he watched as the pulse at the base of her neck increased.

"I think it's time you talk to me, Princess. I know something's been wrong since we left the clubhouse. We're not going a minute longer without talking about it."

Taking her hands, he tugged her out of the closet and into the bedroom. Sitting on the chaise lounge, he pulled her to sit beside him. Holding on to one of her hands, he released the other.

Cupping her face, he made it impossible for her to look anywhere else except at him. He didn't like the anxiousness he read in her expression.

"Whatever it is, we can't get past it until we talk about it. So, tell me what's going on before you give yourself an ulcer."

Her eyelids fluttered closed, and she inhaled deeply. When he initially took her hand, she simply allowed him to hold it. Now, her fingers gripped his. When she finally lifted her lashes to look at him, his eyes were waiting for hers. Encouraging her to say what needed to be said.

"How well do you know Lacey?"

Toad's brow furrowed. That wasn't even close to what he thought she'd say. He almost asked who was Lacey, then he remembered the new chick Kelsey brought in recently to try out as an Angel.

"I don't, other than she's been hanging around the club lately. Why? Did she say something to you?"

"No. Not to me."

"Then who?"

"She was talking to Fubar, but he wasn't interested."

Toad rubbed his thumb along Esmeralda's cheek and slid his fingers around to grasp the back of her neck. Seeing Lacy get the brush off couldn't be all there was to it. As much as he wanted to push, he simply watched and waited. The rest would come. He didn't have long to wait. Similar to when she did a massive download in the parking lot outside of Clive's place, words spilled from Esmeralda's lips.

"You know what kind of work I do. We talked about it. I meet a lot of people. Some I remember. Some I don't. I remember Lacey. Only I don't know her as Lacey. I know her as Agent Deena Hall. FBI agent Deena Hall. She works in a division of the bureau assigned to human trafficking cases.

Is that what you guys are into? If it is, I can't be a part of it. I appreciate you looking out for me and getting my car taken in for new tires. I'll pay for the tow, for the gas, and whatever else you guys have put out helping me, but I can't be around people who have those kinds of ties. I know I shouldn't tell you any of this, but Coral swore it couldn't possibly be true."

It took every ounce of reserve Toad could muster not to rip away from Esmeralda, tear out of her driveway to the clubhouse and toss that rat out on her ass. He didn't for a second doubt the truth of Esmeralda's words. She was too distraught for it to be a lie.

Even as he boiled internally with barely checked rage, he noticed the tears gathering in her eyes. She hadn't wanted to tell him what she'd just said. It was a no-win situation. She didn't really know him well enough to owe him any loyalty. But the fact that she had said anything, told him her pull to him was just as strong as his pull to her.

Although she'd asked the questions, she hadn't wanted to believe the worst of him. He was sure a big part of the reason she trusted him enough to finally spill was due to Coral vouching for the MC.

Swiping at the tears sliding down her cheeks, Toad's mind raced with the things he needed to get done—quickly. First, he had to take care of his woman. Then, he had to get a rodent out of their clubhouse.

"Princess, there will be a lot of shit I can never tell you, but I will tell you this. Sin City doesn't traffic people. We never have and we never will."

Although his gut told him she was certain, Toad asked anyway. "Are you sure the woman you saw was an FBI agent?"

"One hundred percent. I think she recognized me too, because she stopped trying to get Fubar's attention the minute we locked eyes." For the first time, Esmeralda initiated physical contact with him when she latched onto his forearm.

"Be careful with her Xavier. She has connections high up and she's been known to make evidence appear when there wasn't enough to satisfy her. I wouldn't put it past her to plant a false trail if she can't find a real one."

As much as he didn't want to leave Esmeralda, Toad knew he had to get back to the clubhouse. His brothers were very likely in more danger than she was. He pressed a kiss to her forehead.

"Princess, I need to go. Come and lock up."

Taking her phone from his pocket, he quickly entered his phone number and called himself. Once his phone rang, he disconnected and gave her the device back.

"I'll call you later."

Glassy eyes stared back at him. She nodded mutely and followed him. Reminding her again to lock up and set her alarm, Toad laced up his boots and walked out.

He stepped into the garage with his phone in his hand tapping out a message to Artyom. They needed to get on top of this shit immediately.

Fubar had on his business face when Toad approached him. There'd be no talk of what Esmeralda told him out in the open, but Toad's face spoke for him.

"We're heading back to the clubhouse. Now."

No questions were asked as the bikes roared to life. As he backed out of the driveway, the garage door lowered and his cellphone rang. Artyom's voice boomed through the car's speakers.

"You wanna run that shit by me one more time?"

Toad wasn't fazed at the lack of greeting. He immediately gave the VP a recap of what Esmeralda told him. They needed to let King know and get Chip to run Deena Hall's name. Chip was one of the MC brothers with serious hacking skills. Toad didn't call on him often, but he was needed now.

Chapter Fourteen

Esmeralda hadn't seen or heard from Xavier in three days. She wasn't sure what she expected after he and the others sped away from her house, but it hadn't been radio silence. Uncertain if she should make contact with him, she'd done nothing. It was the weekend, and she had no plans, so being without transportation wasn't an issue.

The first morning after he'd left, Esmeralda was awakened by a short text from Xavier letting her know a couple of prospects would be there soon to return her vehicle. The message included a photo of two younger men along with their names.

Minutes later, she received a call from the gate. Once she confirmed their identity, she entered the code. The men didn't attempt to interact with her. They left her SUV in the driveway. She wasn't sure who was who, but the blonde guy got into a second vehicle driven by a man with dark brown hair. The two drove away soon after.

The text was the last form of communication she had with Xavier. Esmeralda wasn't sure how she felt knowing her sole concern was if he was okay. She had no remorse about outing Deena Hall. Her lack of regret was a source of unease. Esmeralda wouldn't characterize herself as heartless, but she really wasn't worried about Deena. Xavier was her concern.

Coral assured her she'd done the right thing. She was so adamant it made Esmeralda curious as to how she could be so certain. The two met because they lived in the same condo complex when Esmeralda moved to Oakland. They became fast friends, and eventually best friends. But there were still parts of their individual lives, before they met, that neither of them knew about.

Coral was an Oakland native, so she was bound to know more about the local MC chapter than Esmeralda. However, her staunch support of them spoke to there being more. As interested as she was, Esmeralda wouldn't push Coral on the subject.

Thoughts of Coral's knowledge of the Sinners was among the others swirling in her mind when Esmeralda parked in the Sin Gym parking lot. She'd spent the time she wasn't worrying about Xavier trying to figure out why anyone would target her. More and more she was beginning to believe the incident with her tires was tied to the other weird things going on around her.

When she returned to work on Monday, the hang ups on her office line had increased to the point she'd begun sending all of her calls to voice-mail. She'd spoken to security, but they were there for building protection, anything else was outside their purview. That didn't make her feel safe.

Grabbing her bag, she looked around as she walked the short distance into the fitness center. Although she didn't expect to see him, her heart sank a little when she walked past the office and through the downstairs area without any sign of Xavier anywhere. While she didn't see him, she did see a few men she was sure were members of the MC.

"You ready to work that core today?"

Coral's face was stretched into a wide smile as she met Esmeralda at the door leading into the studio on the second floor.

"I'm ready to give it a try."

Esmeralda tried to sound optimistic, but the pole dancing class didn't have as much appeal as it had when she attended the previous times.

"You're gonna do more than try, chick."

True to Coral's statement, by the end of the class, sweat was pouring off of Esmeralda. She knew she'd feel the effects of the workout in her stomach muscles for at least a couple of days.

"So, what are you thinking? Shower here then get a bite?"

Coral wiped her face with the towel draped around her neck. Esmeralda checked the time before nodding.

"Sounds fine to me. I brought a change of clothes."

"Cool. Let's hit it."

After they'd showered and changed, the two walked back through the fitness center. Try as she might, Esmeralda couldn't stop herself from looking around. She told herself she wasn't looking for Xavier. He wasn't there, anyway.

Esmeralda and Coral were chatting as they walked toward their vehicles when the squeal of tires drowned out their conversation. Coral just barely managed to pull Esmeralda back before she was hit. A black car with dark tinted windows sped through the parking lot and out into traffic. It came within a hairsbreadth of clipping another vehicle when it shot onto the road.

Not even two seconds later, two men streaked by them. It happened so quickly, the leather of their cuts appeared as unrecognizable black flashes.

"What the FUCK was that?!" Coral's eyes were saucers. With one hand on Esmeralda's shoulder, she peered into her face. "Are you okay?"

"Yeah...Thanks to you."

Esmeralda's voice sounded weak, as her heart thudded in her ears. Adrenaline coursed through her veins while she considered how closely she'd come to being seriously injured or killed. There was no mistaking the driver of the car intended to do her harm.

Her body seemed to vibrate from the hormonal increase and her breathing accelerated. She was cognizant of Coral wrapping an arm around her shoulders, but Esmeralda's body didn't acknowledge the weight of it. *Someone tried to kill her.*

The men who'd run after the car walked back toward them in long strides. One of them held a phone in his hand.

"Ladies, come back inside. Toad is on his way."

Esmeralda had no idea who they were, but she recognized the Sin City MC patches they wore. She didn't have it in her to argue that Xavier Carmichael wasn't in charge of her. Coral hugged her shoulders as they turned back into the building.

They were seated in the office for less than ten minutes when Xavier burst through the door. Coming straight to her, his sharp eyes studied her. It felt like he scanned her for the slightest possible injury. She hadn't even realized she stood up until he gathered her close to him.

"Somebody. Talk. What happened?"

The taller of the two men spoke up. The name, Fox, was stitched onto the patch on his cut.

"It's like I said on the phone. The car came out of nowhere. Then, it sped off—right into traffic. The best I could do was get the plate."

Esmeralda looked up at Xavier's face in time to see him give the man a deadly expression.

"Where the fuck were you?"

"We were right behind her. You told us not to get in the way."

"Don't get in the way doesn't mean let her get hit by a fucking car."

Esmeralda pushed against Xavier's chest. She knew she hadn't misheard, but she still asked, "You had people following me?"

Xavier's arm tightened against her back. His dark eyes were unrepentant as he shifted his gaze to hers.

"Not followed. Protected." Lifting his head, he addressed the others. "Give us the room."

Everyone, including Coral, silently filed out of the room. Esmeralda tried to figure out how she ended up in this situation. A month ago, she'd just learned this man existed and now he was holding her in his arms, refusing to let her go. On top of that, he was having men follow her.

As soon as the door closed behind the last person, Esmeralda looked at Xavier. Her questions were written across her face. Guiding her to a chair, he sat on the edge of the desk in front of her. His long legs bracketed hers. Folding her arms, Esmeralda waited for him to explain himself.

"I don't have to tell you that you're in danger. After what happened on Friday and again today, you're aware. Since I had to handle the situation with Lacey—Deena Hall, I made sure someone was watching your back when I couldn't be there."

"Okay, but why is it your responsibility?"

"It just is, Princess."

His answer wasn't a viable reason to Esmeralda. It was essentially, *'Because I said so'*. Only her parents were able to successfully use that one. But she didn't get a chance to inform him of that fact.

"Have you ever heard of the Elias family? Specifically, Yannis Elias?"

"No... why?"

"Because the case you're working on with the county sheriff might have ties to him. He's the head of a Greek crime family. Word is they're trying to get a foothold in LA."

"What case and how do you know about what I'm working on? I never told you specifics."

"How I know isn't important. What I know is the man, many considered to be an obstacle to Yannis getting what he wants, disappeared months ago. Mauricio's people have been putting up a front like he's okay while they've been quietly trying to find him. His brother is running things in his place, but he's losing his hold on their people."

"That's interesting, but what does it have to do with me?"

"The body found near Mt Diablo was most likely Mauricio. Someone doesn't want it identified or they don't want you to testify as to the identity and possible cause of death."

Esmeralda's heart almost stopped. Pressing a hand to her chest, she stared at the stitching on Xavier's cut. She'd worked countless criminal cases making victim identifications and in some cases assisting with the possible cause of death.

Never had her life been threatened. Not once. Science wasn't supposed to be dangerous. *Was it?*

Chapter Fifteen

Esmeralda looked so shocked and out of sorts, Toad wanted to gather her back into his arms and make all of her worries disappear. Things like this shouldn't touch her, but it was presently their reality.

He'd been busy the last few days. First, he had to deal with how an undercover FBI agent managed to gain entry into their clubhouse. When he'd returned, Lacey was long gone, but Kelsey was still around. Esmeralda was right about the fake Angel. Deena Hall didn't think twice about saving herself and leaving Kelsey out to dry.

Kelsey swore on everything that she had no idea who Lacey really was. It didn't matter though. She'd brought her in—vouched for her. So, she was held responsible. It wasn't the most pleasant part of his role as Sergeant at Arms, but he would protect his brothers. Always.

Three days ago

By the time he made it to the clubhouse, Artyom had already alerted King. All the officers were present, and as many brothers as they could gather on short notice were on hand for this emergency Church.

Instead of sitting, King stood at the head of the table with his arms crossed over his chest. When Toad, Fubar and the others entered the room, there was no delay in getting things started.

"Somebody wanna tell me how the fuck we had a Fed in our clubhouse and no one knew about it?"

King's blue eyes flashed with anger and his already deep voice sounded like a growl. Toad knew he was pissed because the Prez kept running his hand over his goatee.

Toad wished he had answers. He felt like he failed his brothers by not protecting against something like this, but Kelsey was a trusted Angel. She'd been around the club for years. When she vouched for Lacey, no one batted an eye.

Besides, all of their members knew not to discuss club business with a piece of ass—even if they'd been around a while. The meeting was heated as they talked about any possible way the club could be vulnerable.

As it turned out, Agent Hall wasn't quite dedicated enough to do more than give a little head and a hand job here or there. She hadn't made it to any of the brother's rooms.

"Toad, tell me again how you came by this information."

"There was an incident outside of Clive's with my woman—"

"Your woman?" Sitch earned a glare from Toad and King at his interruption. Holding his hands up, he dipped his head in silent apology.

"As I was saying, there was an incident. So, I brought her here with me to get my truck. She was waiting for me outside when she saw Lacey."

"She waited for you outside? By herself?"

"Come on, King. I know better. She was with Frenchie."

All eyes turned to Frenchie who was leaned against the wall on Toad's right. He nodded in agreement.

"We were outside when Lacey came out trying to latch on to Fubar. When Toad's woman saw Lacey, it freaked her out. She didn't say anything, but I could tell."

"If she knew when Lacey was still here, why are we just now hearing about it?"

Toad cursed internally and clenched his jaw. He knew the question was coming, but it didn't make it easier to admit Esmeralda wasn't sure they—no he—could be trusted. It wasn't pretty, but he told them everything. When he was done, at least King nodded in understanding.

As King went, so did the rest of the club. Toad really didn't want to fuck anyone up for talking shit about Esmeralda. It was reasonable for her not be eager to sell out an FBI agent. Especially considering she had to maintain a working relationship with the government.

"Alright." King looked at Fubar. "Bring Kelsey into my office."

Before King could close the meeting, Toad spoke up. "Hey Prez, one more thing. I'd like some guys to help keep an eye on my woman. I don't think what happened to her was random. I know we have to work this shit out with the Feds investigating us, but I want her protected. I just need a few guys until I figure out what's going on."

"Are you officially claiming her?"

Toad had called Esmeralda his woman, out loud, in front of the brothers, but all of them knew having a woman and an Old Lady weren't the same thing. Claiming her in that way was an entirely different ball of wax. Hell, he hadn't even properly kissed her. Was he willing to go that far?

King interrupted Toad's internal debate. "Look. We don't have time to fuck around. We have a lot going on. Aside from each other, we protect family and old ladies. She isn't your blood relative. So, if you want to use club resources, she better damn well be your Old Lady."

Toad's jaw hardened. "Fine. I'm claiming her as my Old Lady."

Knocking against the table, King called for the vote. Only four people in the room had met Esmeralda, but there wasn't one dissenting vote. It warmed Toad to know his brothers had his back even while quite a few of them had their own shit going on.

Esmeralda spoke, pulling him from the memory. "Why would they target me though? I'm just one potential witness."

He couldn't help himself. Toad took one of her hands in his. Rubbing his thumb along the back, he peered into her eyes.

"You don't give yourself enough credit, Princess. Your reputation in the forensics world is impeccable. Do you realize none of the cases you've worked on have had convictions overturned for improper identification?"

Esmeralda's eyes widened. "What? How do you know that?"

Toad shook his head. "You know the internet exists right? A body can find out a lot if they're willing to look for it. Anyone with something to lose wouldn't want you anywhere near a case they didn't want solved."

The anxiousness was still present as her gaze skittered away from his to look at a spot on the wall. He could almost see the wheels turning in her head. Toad didn't think it was necessary to tell her that his *internet search* was actually Chip and his hacking skills getting into records not available to the general public.

When she finally looked at him again, her brown eyes had a dullness to them that Toad didn't like. Almost like defeat. Tugging on her hand, he pulled until she stood between his outstretched legs.

Wrapping his arms around her, he hugged her. Her arms snaked around his waist and Toad damn near sighed from how good it felt to hold her so closely. It was the most natural thing in the world for him to kiss her temple, then her cheek, and finally her plush lips.

"Don't worry, Princess. I've got you."

With his declaration, Toad deepened the kiss. Her lips parted allowing him entry, and he immediately accepted the invitation to explore her mouth. As wonderful as it was to finally taste her, he reluctantly pulled away from the kiss. With parting pecks, he ended it.

"Come on. Let's get out of here. Get you somewhere safe until we can get to the bottom of things."

Chapter Sixteen

Somewhere safe turned out to be Esmeralda's house—with a few modifications and additions from Fubar and Chip. No longer stunned by Fubar's too handsome face, Esmeralda was a bit surprised when she met Chip, who looked more like a football linebacker than a computer nerd.

Between the two of them, Esmeralda doubted a bee would be able to land on one of the flowers on her patio without them knowing about it. The saying, *never judge a book by its cover*, was in full effect when it came to those guys.

Once they left, it was just her and Xavier in the house. Coral had been given an escort home. It was a precaution; although they didn't think she was in any danger.

The roar of the bikes as they exited her street made Esmeralda cringe. She was so going to be hearing from her HOA about that. Xavier's bike was parked in the normally empty spot next to her vehicle in the garage. Despite only having one mode of transportation, she didn't use the extra space for storage.

Xavier's arms wrapped around her from behind and Esmeralda was surprised she wasn't the least bit startled. *Who the hell was this woman she'd turned into overnight?* For the life of her, she couldn't understand how she folded so easily when it came to him. Was it the potential danger and the confidence he exuded?

Goodness knows she'd never been in a position where she had to worry about her well being this way. It bothered her that she thought she was being more diligent after the kidnapping attempt, but she hadn't noticed guys on motorcycles following her. It was downright shameful that she didn't catch on.

"Have you eaten? I'm guessing you burned plenty of calories in Coral's class. You need to replenish."

Something about the way he made the suggestion sounded like a promise she'd need nourishment for other reasons, but it was quite possibly her imagination. She'd become accustomed to the tingling feeling she experienced in his presence, but having him hold her added a layer of intimacy she wasn't certain she was ready for.

It was barely a month from the first time they'd met. Who gets this close to someone so quickly? Not her. It had never happened to her. Even when she thought she was in love in college, she hadn't allowed the kind of liberties Xavier had taken.

The man completely disregarded personal space when it came to her. Apparently, her personal space included him inside it. Shockingly, she didn't mind. She actually found it comforting. Considering the job she loved could be the reason for her life being in danger, she wouldn't begrudge herself the comfort.

"What do you say, Princess? Should I order dinner? Or do you have something here we can whip up?"

Tilting to the side, she looked up over her shoulder at him. "Is that some kind of bid to get me to cook for you?"

"Nope. I know how to feed myself. I'm just trying to see what you prefer. I'd rather not take a chance on delivery, but I can get a Prospect to bring us something. However, if your cupboards are bare, we need to get some groceries."

"Why are you talking as if we'll be holed up here indefinitely?"

Xavier's hands moved to her hips which he used to turn her to face him. "Until we have a handle on what's happening, it's best if you don't go in to the office. Can you work from home?"

Esmeralda pressed against his chest. She couldn't think when they were so close. Shaking her head, she tried to put some distance between them.

"No. I don't have that kind of job. At least I'm not at that stage on anything. I do more than simply write reports."

"Well, you need to figure something out, because you're not going if you aren't safe there."

Heat crawled up Esmeralda's neck and settled in her cheeks. "You don't get to tell me where I can and cannot go, Xavier. How can you imply I'm not safe there? The two times I've been in physical danger have been when I'm nowhere near my office."

The memory of the random phone calls tickled the back of her mind, but she brushed it off.

"Don't get me wrong, I appreciate what you did for me on Friday, and the things the guys did today for my security. But don't get it twisted, none of that gives you a say in my life."

"Woman, you have no idea what it took for me to get you the protection you didn't even know you had."

"I didn't ask you for protection, Xavier!"

"You didn't have to fucking ask! It's what you deserve!"

Scant millimeters separated them. Xavier's eyes were fiercely dark and filled with fire. Esmeralda met his scowl with one of her own. Both of their chests rose and fell as they breathed deeply.

Was he correct when he said she deserved to be protected? Yes. Did it give him the right to bulldoze his way into her life and demand things of her? No. Not in Esmeralda's opinion.

"Maybe you should just leave."

"The fuck I will."

Esmeralda's next words were swallowed by Xavier's kiss. His strong hands cupped her face tilting it up to his. The way he took her lips stole her words and her resolve vanished. A moan escaped when he adjusted them to deepen the kiss.

When they landed on the nearby couch, she gasped at the feel of his scruff against her skin as he kissed his way down her neck. The lightweight blouse she wore was no competition for his seeking fingers. It was unbuttoned and discarded in a matter of seconds—all without breaking the connection between his lips and her body .

Any part of Esmeralda's brain trying to throw up roadblocks or logic was summarily turned off when Xavier's teeth clamped onto her nipple through her bra. The bite wasn't painful. Just the opposite. The pressure was so good arousal flooded her channel and a moan tore from her throat.

His hands weren't the only ones that were busy. Esmeralda's roamed the parts of him she could reach, tugging at the t-shirt covering his muscular torso. Xavier gave her breast a reprieve long enough to yank the shirt over his head and flick the clasp open on her bra.

"Fuck, you're beautiful."

He spoke with such reverence, Esmeralda's breath caught in her throat. The intensity with which he stared at her was its own form of foreplay. When he pushed her breast together and began to worship them alternately, her thoughts scattered and all she could do was feel.

She'd never been into breast play in the past, but it was different with Xavier. It was obvious from the way he kissed, nibbled and sucked on them that he was intent on giving her pleasure.

"I've wanted these beauties in my mouth from the first moment I saw you. Damn, you taste so fucking good. Do you taste good everywhere?"

Xavier didn't give her a chance to answer his question. He gave her breasts a parting kiss and began working his way down her torso, peeling her pants and panties off as he went. Esmeralda squeaked as she was suddenly whirled around with her back against the seat cushions and her ass being held up with Xavier's big hands.

The tip of his nose grazed her exposed mons before she felt the first swipe of his tongue. It made her forget her precarious position on the edge of the sofa. When he coaxed her clit from its hood with a suckling kiss, she forgot her name.

"Fuck!" Her hoarse yell pierced the otherwise quiet of the room. She didn't realize she started to squirm away until Xavier jerked her hips and growled at her.

"Bring that good pussy back here."

His skillful assault on her flower made coherent speech impossible. Single word babble fell from Esmeralda's lips. When he slipped two fingers inside her channel and unerringly found that special place, she was thrown into a leg shaking orgasm.

"Ah, fuck!"

"Mmmm! I like that shit. Do it again." Xavier groaned against her folds.

The words caused a vibration directly to her center. The pre-orgasmic tingles started all over again. Esmeralda was stunned. Being ready for round two had never occurred so quickly, but Xavier was a breaker of all of her boundaries and rules—setting his own precedence.

After he wrung a second orgasm from her, he snatched her into his arms and stood.

"Ooo!" Esmeralda grasped his shoulders as Xavier stalked through the house.

"We need more space." Licking his lips, his eyes captured hers and mesmerized her with the passion banked behind them. "I'm not done with you yet."

Chapter Seventeen

Sexing Esmeralda into submission hadn't been Toad's original plan, but when a good plan presented itself, who was he to turn it away? Her cute little squeal when he picked her up, made him want to carry her around all the time just to hear the sound.

Entering her bedroom, he lowered her to the bed. The entire time, he never broke eye contact. Toad wanted her to stay in the moment. If he gave her too much space, she'd talk herself out of doing what she really wanted. Now that he'd tasted her sweetness, it couldn't happen.

Shucking off the rest of his clothes, he grabbed the condoms he kept in his wallet. There were only two, but he was thankful at least they were there. Standing beside the bed, he stared at her as she watched him roll the latex protection onto his length.

Toad was hard enough to drive nails. Pre-cum gathered at the tip of his shaft. Esmeralda licked her lips and his knees almost buckled imagining their fullness wrapped around his cock. *Later. Much later.* He might let her use her mouth on him. Now, he had to be inside her.

Feeling the tightness of her pussy around his fingers had almost been too much. He had to drive his cock into that velvet paradise. Crawling onto the bed, he spread her legs and settled his hips between them.

Bracing himself with one arm, he notched the tip of his thickness at the opening of her channel.

Her eyes fluttered closed when he pressed in the slightest amount. Looking down to where they were connected, Toad almost lost control. Seeing himself slide inside her while watching his cock disappear between those puffy lips was too much. Slamming his eyes closed, he dropped his forehead to hers. The smell of her signature peach scent assailed his nostrils hardening his length even more.

"You feel so fucking good, Princess." He flexed his hips driving himself deeper within her walls drawing a gasp from Esmeralda. "Mmm... Don't be shy. You can tell me how much you like having my dick sliding inside your sweet pussy."

Lifting his eyelids, he took her lips again in a kiss mimicking the movements of his length with his tongue before pulling away with parting pecks. As soon as he released her lips, the keening pants started up.

"It's okay, Princess. It's just the two of us. You can talk as filthy as you want. I won't judge."

The bite of her nails digging into his flank made Toad close his eyes briefly to revel in how good that shit felt. The softness of her skin was doing a number on his senses already.

Adjusting their position, he lifted her left leg, propping it on his shoulder allowing him even more depth into her delicious pussy. He swiveled his hips. The motion earned him more than single incoherent words from his princess.

"Oh Fuck! Just like that!"

Grinning, Toad did it again. He had to give the lady what she asked for. "Just like that, sweetheart? Any other requests?"

A sheen of sweat covered them and he couldn't resist licking the column of Esmeralda's neck. Licking escalated to sucking, uncaring if he left a mark. He apparently pressed the magic button.

Esmeralda released a string of curses followed by how good his dick felt stretching her tight pussy. He almost came when she told him his dick was so pretty she wanted to suck him dry, but it was so big she had to have him inside her or she would go crazy.

As she talked, she tilted her hips into his thrusts and her walls seemed to undulate around his shaft. Her nails were short and blunt, yet he still felt the sting of them digging into his forearms as she screamed that she was cumming.

"Fuck yeah, Princess! Come all over my cock. I want your sticky sweetness all over me."

Esmeralda's body stiffened and her channel locked down on his cock so hard, Toad had no choice but to fall with her into nirvana. His hips jerked spastically as he emptied himself into the condom—wishing there wasn't a barrier between them.

Breathing heavily, he lowered her leg and reluctantly withdrew from her heated core. His dick twitched like it didn't appreciate being forced to leave the sweet haven. *I know buddy. It's fucking heaven.* Toad gave it a silent pep talk.

Unwilling to separate from her completely, he tugged her into his arms. They could clean up in a few. He wasn't ready for anything to pierce their bubble. Apparently, Esmeralda was in agreement. Her fingers lazily stroked one of his arms.

Soon, her even breathing told him she'd drifted off to sleep. Toad fought sleep long enough to clean them both up and tuck her beneath the covers. Grabbing his phone from the living room, he shot a message to Artyom. His MC brother owned a restaurant Toad trusted. And the food was good. Once he was assured a prospect would be over with dinner, Toad cuddled Esmeralda close and joined her in slumber.

Not much of a napper, he didn't sleep long. He awakened in time to buzz the prospect through the gate to bring their dinner. As he finished laying the food out on the dining room table, a groggy Esmeralda appeared in the doorway rubbing her eyes like a toddler. *Why was that shit so cute?*

"Hey there, Princess. You're just in time for dinner."

Pulling out a chair, Toad seated her before sitting in the one across from hers. She stared at the offering with wide eyes.

"What's all this?"

"Russian food from my brother's place."

Esmeralda's nose crinkled slightly. "Do you not like Russian food?"

"I haven't eaten it much, but I don't dislike it."

"So, what was the face about?"

"What face?"

Moving his finger in a circle, Toad pointed at her nose. "The one that had your nose scrunched when I said what kind of food this was."

Esmeralda's eyebrows shot up and the cute little wrinkle on the bridge of her nose disappeared.

"That wasn't a face-face. It was me trying to figure out what each dish was and if I'd had it before."

Leaning on his elbows, Toad pointed to each container. "Here we have, Blinchiki, stuffed crepes. These have meat in them, but they can come with veggies as well."

As he described the remaining items, he began loading a plate adding or skipping an option based on her expression when he described it. The entire scenario reminded him of his parents. He was gonna have to call them soon to check on them.

Once he placed a full plate in front of her, he quickly prepared one for himself. A comfortable silence stretched between them as they consumed the delicious meal. Toad had a hearty appetite and was happy to see Esmeralda didn't shy away from eating.

When they were done, Toad folded his arms and pierced her with his direct stare. Instead of looking him in the face, her eyes were glued to his chest. He'd only slipped on pants when he left her in bed, so his bare chest was on display.

"Do all of your tattoos mean something?" The crinkle in her nose was back—accompanied by the lifting of one arched eyebrow.

Looking down at his torso then his arms, Toad took stock of his ink. Some of it had been there before he moved to Oakland, but there were some additions courtesy of Saint's talented hands.

"No. Not all of them. But some do. Some I got just because I was young, wild, and stupid."

"La Vida Loca?"

"Wild youthful moment."

"The cross? Are you religious?"

"Not particularly. I *was* called a demon once, though."

"Okay..." Esmeralda propped her chin on her hand as she continued to rake her gaze over him. Everywhere her eyes touched sparked a low simmering blaze beneath his skin.

"What about the 1983?"

Her question doused the flame with ice cold water. He'd discovered pretty early on he couldn't lie to her. But, he wasn't ready to talk about the reason for that particular piece.

"So, what's the story? More wild youth? Were you even born then?"

"Yes, I was born then. I was actually born in '81." Chuffing, Toad shook his head. "You have the nerve to ask me if I was born then like I'm some kid and you weren't even born until '87. Of the two of us, you're the child."

"If I'm a child, you're robbing the cradle."

"So be it. I robbed it and I'm keeping the spoils."

Reaching across the table, he ran a finger over her forearm. Her skin was so soft and she smelled so delectable, he had a hard time not touching her. Toad was surprised he'd made it through the meal without pulling her into his lap. Now that they'd ventured into physical intimacy, the gloves were off. He'd touch her whenever he damn well pleased.

Chapter Eighteen

Esmeralda's head spun trying to categorize what was happening in her life. Her boring, humdrum existence had been turned on its ear. For the sake of keeping the peace, she'd taken off for the past three days, but she needed to get back into the office. There was a meeting scheduled to discuss her identification of the remains she'd been working on and she had others which required her attention. A few that she'd been specifically requested to work on.

In her home office, she typed away on a report to send to Olga to add to the others regarding an assignment she'd completed weeks ago. She guessed one positive resulted from this lockdown Xavier had her in—she was catching up on paperwork. She was on the edge though. They weren't any closer to figuring out why someone would want to kidnap or harm her.

Xavier was convinced it was connected to the LA crime syndicate, but Esmeralda wasn't. Why would someone not want her to identify the remains of a crime boss? Weren't there always bloody leadership turnovers in the mafia-type world? It stood to reason they'd want conclusively to know the man was dead so there wasn't a looming threat to the new boss.

Besides, the attempts to get to her were clumsy and not well thought out. People familiar with criminal dealings would have taken her out much more quickly. It was a morbid thought, but Esmeralda was realistic. A crime syndicate could make her disappear without a trace. That's the other reason she wasn't sold on the whole *the Greeks were after her* scenario.

"Hey, Princess. I have something for you to look at. Tell me if you recognize anyone."

Xavier entered her office with an electronic tablet in his hand. Esmeralda didn't look directly at him, because she apparently couldn't do that without hopping on his dick. She'd learned her lesson a couple of days ago when he had to make a midnight run to get more condoms. They'd exhausted both his and her supply on hand. Accepting the device, she looked at the images on the screen.

A nugget of thought tickled the back of her mind when she looked at the man on the display, but she couldn't place him. The jawline was familiar, but beyond that, Esmeralda had nothing.

"I don't know who this is."

Using his thumb and pointer finger, Xavier zoomed in on the image. "Take a good look."

Esmeralda stared at the closer image for a few beats. She got the same niggling feeling, but she still came up empty. Shaking her head, she tried to pass the tablet back to him.

"I'm sorry. I don't recognize him. Where is this photo from?"

"Right outside your office building." Pushing the device back to her, he swiped to the next image. "What about this one?"

They continued the same process for a few more pictures. Esmeralda was about ready to scream when she realized something. She wasn't being shown photos of multiple people, she was being shown multiple pictures of the same person. The clothing changed along with the cut and color of the hair, but the facial structure was the same.

Whoever the guy was even went through the trouble of doing things to look different heights and body weights, but the face was the same. Even beneath the mustache and beard combinations, she discerned the uniqueness of the man's jaw line. Considering she made her living analyzing skeletal remains, she was a little disappointed it took her so long to hone in on it.

"Wait! This is the same guy."

Xavier leaned in closer. "So, you do recognize him?"

"No. I don't know him, but I'm positive this is the same person. He's just wearing different clothes and putting on wigs and fake facial hair."

Esmeralda started to ask Xavier how he came to have pictures of people coming and going from her office building, but thought better of it. Plausible deniability and all that.

Taking the tablet, Xavier pressed a kiss to her cheek, stood up straight, and walked out.

"Well... Okay then...Nice talk."

Esmeralda spoke to the empty room, because not even Xavier's shadow graced the entryway. Returning to her computer, she refocused on her report. The image on the screen didn't completely leave her thoughts, but she was able to get the remainder of her work done.

"So, do you think you'll be in on Monday? I can check the rest of the team's schedule and pick a time that best suits yours."

"I'll be there, but don't try to get anyone to re-arrange their schedules to suit me. I'll figure something out."

"It's really not a problem."

"Olga. I'm serious. Do not make those people move stuff to accommodate me. I'll work it out on my end."

Silence was Olga's response for a solid minute before she murmured a quiet, "Okay."

Esmeralda was happy to have Olga for an assistant. She kept things on task and no one got past her unless Esmeralda wanted them there. Esmeralda would sooner quit than give up Olga.

Wrapping up the call, she stood from her desk and stretched. It was Friday, and she'd been cooped up in her house for almost a solid week. Okay, cooped up was a bit of a stretch. She did leave, but only when Xavier was with her. When she asked him how he could afford to be away from his business and the club for so long, he informed her people were trained to do certain tasks for a reason. That was it. End of discussion.

There was a chiming ding when Esmeralda opened the door leading to the sunporch at the back of her house. She initially wanted a patio, but she also didn't want to fight insects every night. The screened in space was her compromise.

Thanks to the position of her house, the porch was shaded in the afternoon. The outdoor space was her small oasis with her potted plants, lounge furniture, and hidden speakers to play her music. She'd no sooner propped her feet on the lounger than the door opened and Xavier walked out.

Forgetting she wasn't supposed to look directly at him, Esmeralda's eyes swept from the tips of his shoes up to his head topped with slightly disheveled sandy colored hair. His biceps bulged beneath the short-sleeved t-shirt and his thighs begged her to sit on them while those sinful lips encircled her nipples. The peaks in question pebbled at the memory of the last time he'd pleasured them.

"Hey, all done for the day?"

Either he didn't know or didn't care how he affected her. Lifting her legs, he sat on the lounger and draped her limbs across his lap. Esmeralda's breath hitched at the skin-to-skin contact created by his shorts riding up his thighs and his palms resting on her calves.

"Um...Yeah. I'm done."

"That's good."

Xavier caressed her lower legs in circles slowly moving upwards. While not completely callused, his fingers and palms bore some signs of his life lifting weights and gripping the handles of his motorcycle. The roughness sent tingles skating along Esmeralda's spine and coalescing at her center.

"I'm done too. I've checked in at the gym and with the brothers at the club. So, nothing for me to do tonight."

The circular motion of his touch ceased beneath her loose dress just as he reached the apex of her legs.

"Nothing except you, that is."

Reflexively, Esmeralda's thighs clamped, mimicking the tightening of her core. The way she responded to him was absolutely insane. She'd never felt anything like it. Xavier's dark eyes sussed out her unspoken desires and his lips claimed hers while his fingers pushed her panties aside and delved between her folds.

A moan tore from Esmeralda's throat. The way he stroked her pearl had her on the edge of orgasm in less than a minute. She'd be ashamed if she didn't know he was good for at least two more before he even let her feel the anaconda he called a dick.

Xavier kissed his way down her jaw to her neck where he latched on. He'd found that spot the first time they'd had sex. Now, he attacked it ruthlessly to send her flying over the edge whenever he wanted. It felt so fucking good, she couldn't even be mad.

Just as she crested achieving her first orgasm, Xavier removed his fingers and dispensed with her underwear. In the space of two breaths, he whirled them around on the lounger with her straddling his legs. Closing her eyes, Esmeralda relished the feeling of Xavier's thickness stretching her walls.

"Fuck, Princess. That pussy missed me didn't she?"

Too far gone to answer, Esmeralda's head rocked back. She didn't have the bandwidth to remind him of their morning activities nor the ones from the night before. Besides, he was right. It's why she couldn't look at him too long. Whenever she did, she was guaranteed to end up onto his dick.

She couldn't blame herself though. Xavier Carmichael was a potent drug and a hell of a ride.

Chapter Nineteen

When Esmeralda's slick walls closed around his length, Toad's eyes slammed shut. He couldn't look at her. If he did, he'd blow his load before the first thrust of his hips. It only took a millisecond to realize the difference in the feeling was due to nothing separating them. *It was fucking amazing.*

Those lush hips, drawing his hands to them like magnets, began a rotation that glided her delicious pussy along his shaft. Giving his digits free rein, Toad clamped onto the rounded cheeks of her ass. Her silky-smooth skin beneath his palms added to the ecstasy of her velvet core rippling along his cock with each stroke.

Gritting his teeth, Toad opened his eyes to the vision of her bountiful breasts jiggling in his face. Unable to resist, he lavished attention on the turgid peaks and rained kisses on both pillowy globes.

"Fuck, baby. You feel amazing. Bounce that ass and take my cock."

Just as he expected, Esmeralda's channel clamped down more on his shaft. A soft gasp was followed by her redoubled efforts to wring every ounce of cum from his balls. She was fucking the shit out of him and he loved every second of it. Having his good girl let go and pant dirty words into his ear was a powerful aphrodisiac.

"Oh shit, Xavier!"

"What is it, Princess? Tell me."

Toad's voice was gravelly and desperate in his desire to hear her describe how she felt. Esmeralda didn't disappoint. His princess had a filthy little mouth. He loved it. Fuck. He loved *her.*

"Damn, Xay. This dick is top tier. I'm so wet, I'm gonna flood this porch."

Twining his fingers in her hair, he pulled her face to his and growled. "Then gush. Drown my cock in your sticky sweet cream."

To help her get there, Toad latched onto the special spot on her neck and pinched her nipples. Meeting her downward glide with upward thrusts, he groaned at the way her pussy devoured his length. It didn't take much more for them both to topple over into the abyss.

Toad's cock jerked within her spasming walls releasing jet after jet of cum into her channel. *Fuck. That felt amazing*. There was no way he could go back to having a barrier between them.

They'd shared their test results days ago, but this was the first time they'd come together without a prophylactic. It wouldn't be the last. Not if he had anything to say about it.

~

"This is a bad idea."

"No, it's not. I have to go back to the real world at some point, Xavier."

"Yes. It is."

Toad buttoned his dark blue slacks and threaded a black leather belt through the loops. Esmeralda was standing before the mirror mounted on the wall wearing a figure-hugging dress which stopped just below her knees. Next to her were the heels she'd selected to match. Her hair was swept into a riot of curls atop her head.

She looked smart, sexy and put together. As he watched her, all he wanted to do was fuck her and muss her neat appearance. But he couldn't. He'd promised she could return to her regular life—with some modifications.

There was a meeting she insisted required her attendance, since she was the senior analyst on the project. Why they called it a project, he didn't know. They analyzed human remains. However, she said they only referred to them as cases when they worked with law enforcement—since in those instances an official case number was assigned.

His gaze drifted to the outfit hanging on the outside of the door to her walk-in closet. It was a creation mainly made of leather including a bustier, and a skirt with a gladiator appearance. Toad knew a large part of her wanting to return to her daily life was because she had tickets to the upcoming Comic Con. She'd been planning it for months.

Although he understood, if the threat to her wasn't resolved, he couldn't get behind her being in such a large crowd of costumed potential attackers. But, the crestfallen look on her face when he told her she might have to miss it, made Toad want to scour the city with a flashlight looking for the son of a bitch who dared to put her safety at risk.

They made it to her office a half hour before foot traffic around the building picked up. One of the conditions of her returning to her regular life was an escort. Him. Despite the privacy surrounding her work, she'd somehow convinced her manager to allow him access to the offices.

Toad had also tapped Fox and a couple of prospects to keep eyes on the outside of the building. He'd bet good money the disguised stalker would be there at some point during the week. They exited the elevator on Esmeralda's floor. Toad felt the stares of her co-workers as they walked toward her office.

He saw them and he heard the murmurs, but he never turned his head to look at anyone. While he was in dress slacks and a button down, he was aware those items of clothing did nothing to camouflage his bulk. His demeanor was purposefully stern and off-putting. And it worked. No one said a word to them until they came abreast of the desk belonging to Esmeralda's assistant, Olga.

"Good morning, Esmeralda and...Oh! Hello. I don't believe we've met." Standing the petite blond extended a hand.

"I'm Olga. Esmeralda's personal assistant."

"I know." Toad shook her hand and released it quickly.

Esmeralda swatted his bicep. He looked down at her with a raised eyebrow which conveyed his unspoken question. *What?*

"Be nice." Turning to Olga, Esmeralda rubbed the same appendage she'd abused and introduced him. "This is Xavier. What he meant to say was I told him all about you."

Toad said exactly what he meant to say, but he didn't correct her. Instead, when Olga looked at him again, he nodded curtly, then returned to scanning the area.

"Okay. Well, I have some messages for you." In old school fashion, Olga passed Esmeralda a small stack of honest to goodness message sheets.

"Thanks." Esmeralda tucked the pink pages into the side of her bag. "I'm going to get settled before my meeting. It's at 9:30 correct?"

"It is." Olga moved her chair to take her seat, but popped back up. "Oh, Esmeralda. I thought you should know. I had your line forwarded to mine, and I kept getting weird hang ups or calls where they didn't say anything. I remember you mentioning something about it last month. Was it still happening to you?"

Toad didn't miss the guilty expression on Esmeralda's face before she cleared it.

"Don't worry about it. Someone has too much time on their hands."

Turning stiffly, she walked swiftly to her office. Unlocking the door, she went inside. Stepping through the opening she left for him, Toad closed the door behind him and turned the lock.

"Do you want to tell me what she's talking about and why you just lied to her?"

Before she spoke, Toad could tell she was going to deflect if not outright lie to him. Moving into her space, he captured her full attention tilting her face up to his.

"Don't even think about lying to me, Esmeralda. What the fuck has been going on here and why didn't you tell me?"

The soft gasp wasn't the same as the ones she uttered when they made love. No. This one was more shock with a tinge of hurt. He knew why. It was rare for him to call her by her name, but he needed her to know how serious he was.

"I didn't say anything because I thought it was some kids or someone with too much time on their hands playing on the phone."

"Don't give me that bullshit. You're too smart to think something like that. Maybe before the first attempt, but not after. After, you had to know there could be some kind of connection, but you didn't say anything."

"Why would I think there was a connection? You're convinced an organized crime family is behind all of this. How many crime syndicates do you know making hang up calls? You can't have this both ways, Xavier. Either it's a professional hit or not. I can't be jumping at my shadow. It's too much."

Toad gritted his teeth and released her from his hold. If he continued to touch her, he might shake her in frustration. For someone so brilliant, she was missing the entire point. Granted she made a valid assessment. The attempts to kidnap and run her down were amateurish.

Still. He hardened his jaw. Esmeralda should've told him about the calls. It was something Chip could run down for them. With that in mind, he pulled out his phone. Opening the door, he pierced her with a censuring stare.

"I'll be back in a few. Do not try to leave this building without me."

"Where am I going, Xavier? I have a meeting in less than an hour, remember?"

"I said what I said." Toad clamped his lips and exited the office. He didn't plan to go far. Just far enough for him to make a couple of calls without being overheard.

Chapter Twenty

Esmeralda looked around the conference room. The people gathered were a mix of *Identalysis* analysts and potential family members of the remains she'd worked to identify over a month ago. The meeting was a measure to bring the entire family up to speed.

Celeste Montague had requested remains previously classified as a Jane Doe by the medical examiner be re-examined by their team in hopes of determining if the deceased was actually her sister, Melisandre, who'd been missing for the past seven years. Esmeralda knew things were going to get messy.

It was inevitable. Braxton Cartwright had been seen all over the city and in photos with his wife—or at least someone who looked like his wife. Celeste wasn't convinced. And, honestly, Esmeralda was inclined to believe her before the team began working on the skeletal remains from the medical examiner.

However, after they were done, Esmeralda was positive. Whoever the woman was parading around Oakland with Braxton, she wasn't Melisandre Montague-Cartwright. Whether it was plastic surgery or a real-life doppelgänger, that woman was a fraud. She was also suspiciously absent from the gathering.

"If everyone is present, we can get started."

Esmeralda tapped the table to get their attention. As project lead, it was her job to give the results and provide whatever information may be required to turn over to the proper authorities. Celeste looked from the door to Braxton.

"I thought Melisandre was coming. Her being here could make this entire thing unnecessary."

"I've already told you. This debacle has given your sister terrible migraines, and she's unable to leave her bed. I can't believe you're putting your family through this." Braxton folded his arms in a huff tipping his nose in the air as if he smelled something foul.

"Well, if you hadn't kept her from us for the past two years, we wouldn't be here would we, Braxton? What are you hiding that my sister can't visit with her family? Our father died, and she wasn't even at the funeral. He was our last surviving parent. My *real* sister would never not be there for her own father's funeral."

"I'm sick of your accusations, Celeste. I've tried all this time to spare your feelings, but I'll just come out and say it. Melisandre no longer wants anything to do with your family. She's so distraught about all of this, I had to have a nurse with her while I'm here."

"That's a load of shit!"

"Okay! That's enough."

Esmeralda cut across what was likely a regular argument between the two. Giving them pointed glances she looked at her manager. Normally, Robert wouldn't attend a wrap up. However, since Esmeralda had the feeling things might go sideways, she'd invited him. Nodding to Olga, she gave her assistant the go ahead to distribute the physical copies of the reports to the family.

Typically, only the client who hired them got a copy, but Celeste was adamant each family member present received one. So, her brother, brother-in-law, aunt and uncle all received a dossier.

Tapping the keyboard in front of her, Esmeralda summarized the content of the files for those present. There was detailed analysis and breakdown, but what it boiled down to was simple.

"In conclusion, the remains received from the medical examiner have been conclusively determined to be those of Melisandre Montague-

Cartwright. With a variance of a week less or more, she has been deceased for seven years and three months."

A loud wail pierced the quiet of the room. The elder Mr. Montague comforted the aunt while Celeste cried quietly into her hands. Her brother, Gabriel, stared at Braxton with murder in his eyes.

"This is preposterous! There is no way this is accurate! Melisandre is home with a migraine! Are you trying to tell me the woman in my home is an imposter?"

Esmeralda had the presence of mind to hit the button for security just before Gabriel flew over the table. He rained blows on Braxton so quickly, he'd split the man's lip and put a cut above his eye before Robert and two others were able to pull him away.

Security arrived with Xavier on their heels. He'd wanted to be inside the room, but there were some rules even she couldn't get Robert to break. Only those approved by the client were allowed inside the conference room. Xavier's sharp gaze raked over her. She put up one hand assuring him she was okay.

"I'm fine! I'm fine. You don't have to guard me. I'll find out another way what that piece of shit did to my sister." Gabriel shrugged of the security guards.

Braxton's words were muffled as he held a handkerchief to his bleeding lip. "I didn't do anything to your sister. I've been deceived just like you have. I thought the woman I'd been sharing my life with for nearly the last two years was the same woman I married. I've been living with a stranger and you're attacking me! I love Melisandre. I'd never do anything to hurt her."

"Liar!" Celeste shrieked. "She was going to divorce you. She told me so right before she disappeared. You knew. Just like you knew after seven years we could declare her dead and you would be cut off from the family trust. That's why you had someone pose as her. But you knew we wouldn't be fooled, so you made up excuses and never let her near any of us."

Holding up his hands, Braxton looked sincerely mortified. "Celeste, I promise you on my mother's grave. I had no idea the woman who returned to me wasn't Melisandre. I'm just as devastated as you. How could I be deceived like this?"

Grabbing the dossier, Celeste stuffed it inside her tote bag. "Thank you, Dr. Upton. Thank you and your team. I will be in touch regarding turning all original information over to the authorities. They'll need it to prosecute my sister's murderer." Tossing Braxton a final glare, she ushered her family from the conference room. Robert escorted them out while security took Braxton to the men's room to get cleaned up.

"Tell me again how your job isn't dangerous." Xavier said once the room was cleared out.

Esmeralda's hands shook slightly as she gathered her things. Although she hadn't been physically involved in the altercation, her adrenaline spiked and now she was coming down. Xavier took the electronics from her and wrapped an arm around her waist.

"Come on, Princess. Let's get you back to your office."

On their way down the corridor created by the cubical walls, Xavier's phone dinged. Hanging back, he nudged her toward her open doorway. Taking her laptop from him, Esmeralda walked the short distance to her office.

Entering she closed the door behind her. When she turned around, her breath caught in her throat. The laptop hit the floor in a muted thud as she raised her hands. Standing next to her desk, was Braxton Cartwright —with a gun. He aimed the weapon at her with a sneer on his face.

"I'm fucking ruined, and it's all your fault. You're going to fix this, or it'll be the last time you interfere in anyone else's life."

Chapter Twenty-One

Toad stepped into an empty office to take the call from Chip. He'd finished running the images through facial recognition based on the parameters Esmeralda had given. Based on her feedback, he focused on the jaw line.

"The guy's name is Braxton Cartwright. He's supposed to be a businessman, but he's really just a high-end grifter. The only thing he managed to not fuck up was getting married to Melisandre Montague. She's an heiress to Montague wine makers."

The rest of what Chip said fell on deaf ears as Toad ended the call and bolted down the hall to Esmeralda's office. Olga looked up curiously when he shot past her and opened the door. There was no one inside and Esmeralda's laptop lay on the floor just inside the entryway.

"Fuck!"

Olga called out to him asking what was wrong as he rushed past her desk and into the nearest stairwell. He managed to call Fox on his way.

"Fox, get eyes on every exit out of this place. That bastard has Esmeralda."

"What bastard?" Fox asked, but Toad heard him directing the prospects to move in and pay attention to everyone trying to leave.

"The one who's been stalking her. I'm coming down the stairs. He'll probably try to take her out through the garage, so send someone to that entrance and you take the other side."

"You got it brother."

Toad's heart raced as he took the stairs two and three at a time, at one point jumping the remaining distance. He hadn't been separated from her long enough for them to be too far ahead. Especially if they took the elevator. He was in the only stairwell not tied to the emergency system. Had they taken the emergency exit, the alarm would've gone off. He was confident and hopeful Cartwright was dumb enough to use the elevator.

As he pushed his way through the heavy door on the bottom level leading to the adjacent parking garage, Toad heard the ding of the elevator. Racing toward the sound, he skidded to a stop as Esmeralda stepped out. Her stiff carriage was the only indicator he needed to know that she was being coerced.

Toad's blood boiled as he looked over her shoulder to see Braxton close behind. When the other man saw Toad standing there, he pulled Esmeralda closer using her as a human shield. He was already a dead man walking for touching her, but by using her to protect himself, Braxton had just ensured his death wouldn't be quick and painless. No. He'd suffer before Toad put him out of his misery.

"You have one chance to leave here alive. Let her go and toss the gun away."

Total lie. But Toad sold it by sounding much calmer than he actually was. With his hands held aloft in surrender, he shifted with each shuffle Braxton made to get away.

"I have a counteroffer. If you don't want her to get hurt. You get out of our way. Once she's done what I need, I'll let her go."

Tipping his head to the side, Toad dropped his hands. "Somehow, I don't believe you, Mr. Cartwright."

"So, you know who I am? Good." The sweaty little shit had the nerve to look smug. Straightening his shoulders, he stood taller behind Esmeralda's shorter frame.

"If you know who I am, then you know that I know people. People who could make your life hell if you don't get out of my way."

"Can't do that."

Esmeralda's wide eyes pleaded with Toad through a sheen of tears. When the first drop of wetness hit her cheek, it took everything in him not to lose his shit.

"You can and you will. Unless you want me to put holes in the pretty doctor lady. This could've been avoided if she'd just ignored my meddling in-laws. Now she has to make it right. Once she does, I'll let her go."

"You must think I'm as dumb as you look." Toad watched Fox move into position behind Cartwright. He was done playing around. Nodding at Fox, he gave him the go ahead to rush Cartwright from behind. As soon as Fox put a hand on him, Toad snatched Esmeralda away and shoved her behind him.

In a matter of seconds, they'd disarmed the other man and had him prostrate on the pavement. When he started to protest too loudly, Toad grabbed his overly long hair and banged his head against the concrete knocking him unconscious. Esmeralda's squeak was the only sound following that action.

Hopping up, Toad approached her pulling her into his arms. He didn't spare a glance for Braxton Cartwright who was likely bleeding from the new opening in his skull. Grateful the enforcers had developed a type of short hand, he only had to look at Fox for him to know what to do next.

The prospects kept watch to make sure no one entered the area and Fox got on the phone to Chip to get the footage wiped. Holding Esmeralda to his chest with one hand, Toad pulled out his phone. Frenchie answered on the second ring.

"Talk."

"I have a mess. I need Keisha."

"Where?"

Toad rattled off the address and Frenchie hung up the phone. Toad didn't worry that his request wouldn't be honored. His brother had his back. Leaving a prospect behind, Toad bundled Esmeralda into his truck. A few minutes later, their package was wrapped and loaded into the bed of the vehicle and they drove away.

Esmeralda didn't say a word as they were parked in his reserved spot in front of Sin Gym. She blinked in surprise as Coral rushed out and pulled on the passenger door, but she didn't say anything. He'd sent Coral a text letting her know Esmeralda needed her.

Helping Esmeralda down, Toad nodded in Fox's general direction. He didn't need words for him to know to keep an eye on the pickup while Toad took care of his woman. It was only when he kissed her forehead and made to leave that Esmeralda seemed to come alive.

Delicate fingers gripped his shirt and held on with more strength than he realized she possessed.

"Where are you going?"

"I can't tell you, Princess. But, I'll be back soon."

"Why can't you tell me? What are you gonna do?"

"I'm going to make sure you never have to worry about Braxton Cartwright again."

Esmeralda's eyes widened, and she shook her head vigorously. "No, Xavier. No. He's not worth it. Let's just turn him in. I don't want this blowing back on you."

Cupping her face, Toad tilted her chin up enough to allow him to capture her lips in a gentle kiss. "Don't you worry about me. I promise, when I'm done, even your brilliant mind won't be able to put together what happened. It'll be like Braxton Cartwright never existed."

"Xavier. Please."

"Princess. You probably know there's very little I wouldn't do for you. But, this is one argument you won't win. There's no way in hell I'm letting a man threaten the woman I love, then hold her at gun point and not suffer the consequences. That ain't the Sinner's way, baby."

With those parting words, he pressed a hard kiss on her lips, turned on his heels and left the room. His mind had already moved on to the man trussed up like hunted prey in the bed of his truck. Braxton Cartwright would pay for terrorizing Esmeralda—then he'd breathe his last breath.

By the time Toad turned onto the road to the seemingly abandoned warehouse a few bikes had fallen in behind him. When he saw Frenchie's Indian, Toad tried to recall if he'd told him anything beyond his request for Keisha's special cleaning services. Pulling his truck behind the building, Toad stepped out with purpose.

Opening the tailgate, he cursed when he saw the condition of the liner. He'd have to see if Keisha could work her magic there as well. Although Braxton's head wound had stopped bleeding, there was blood streaked on the liner along with a puddle of urine. Motherfucker had pissed himself.

Motorcycles rumbled next to his truck. Toad nodded to the prospects, and in a few minutes Cartwright was taken inside the building, untied, then strapped to a straight back wooden chair.

Eyes bulging in fear, he stared at the group of rough looking men gathered around him in a wide arc. Toad stood directly before him taking stock of the damage already done. He didn't waste time keeping his promise about making Cartwright suffer.

The fingers he'd used to dial Esmeralda's number and touch her without permission were broken—individually. Toad allowed a minute in between to really let the pain settle in. When Cartwright fainted from the agony, Toad revived him.

"Nah...You don't get to sleep through your punishment. Wake your ass up."

"Please...Please stop. I'll give you whatever you want. I have money."

Toad didn't bother responding to the pleas. Done with the fingers, he released Cartwright's right arm, extended it out straight, and brought an elbow down on the joint that connected it to the man's shoulder. He'd touched Esmeralda there to shove her in front of himself.

Every place the other man dared to touch his woman was etched into Toad's memory. He methodically worked his way through meting punishment for the infractions. No one helped, but no one stopped him either. When it was all said and done, Braxton Cartwright was completely unrecognizable and wouldn't have been capable of walking away even if they removed the restraints.

"You done?"

Frenchie's question pulled Toad out of the darkness he'd descended into. Toad looked at his MC brother.

"Why? You wanna give him last rites or some shit?"

Frenchie lifted one eyebrow, his expression said, *Fuck No.*

"If you're done, he needs to disappear."

Toad nodded in agreement. Cartwright's head hung limply on his shoulders and small whimpers passed through his lips. No sympathy was given. Besides what he'd tried to do to Esmeralda, it was quite likely he'd killed his wife and replaced her with a fake to keep her money. He didn't deserve pity. Instead, Toad walked behind the chair, grabbed Cartwright's head and snapped his neck like a twig.

Chapter Twenty-Two

Esmeralda stood in front of her full-length mirror regarding the woman in the reflection. It was her, but it wasn't. Her skin seemed to glow more golden brown against the black leather of the outfit she wore. Her normally full breasts were pushed up high by the leather bustier and her waist was cinched by the tightly laced corset.

Well, it wasn't laced too tightly, Xavier refused to go tighter. He said she was already perfect. In his words, there was no reason to cut off her air supply. A smile tugged at the corner of Esmeralda's lips as she thought about how hard it was to get him to even lace her up when all he seemed to be interested in was removing the costume altogether.

The past few weeks following the incident with Braxton Cartwright had been interesting to say the least. After Xavier dropped her off at the gym Esmeralda didn't know what to think. She was terrified for him. Not because she thought it was remotely possible for Braxton to hurt him, but because of the implications of what he'd told her when he walked away.

He had every intention of killing a man. For her. It was brain bending. And to top it off, while he promised to end a man's life on her behalf, he professed his love for her. He'd done it in such a matter-of-fact way, it had taken almost an hour for it to sink in. During that time, she'd nearly worn a hole in the carpet of his office pacing.

When Fubar and two prospects came to escort her home, she was almost distraught thinking the worst. She was so on edge, when Xavier pulled into her driveway on his Harley, she raced outside in her bare feet and threw herself into his arms.

After she checked every inch of him for damage to his person, she spent the rest of the night professing and displaying her love for him. They'd been inseparable ever since. Xavier told her he'd been debating on purchasing a house, but he'd lived at the club house because he felt it was best to be close by in case his brothers needed him. Now that they were together, he was more adamant that they needed their own space. He still kept his rooms at the clubhouse. They'd stayed a few nights there after partying so hard it wasn't safe to drive back to her place afterwards.

A giggle bubbled up and escaped Esmeralda's lips. Who would've thought she would be partying with bikers and loving every second of it? She'd even gotten over having the Angels around. She only had to put one of them in her place before the rest got the message. Xavier was off the market.

"What are you giggling about, Princess Peach?"

Xavier's strong arms slid around her, hugging her back to his front. Kissing her exposed shoulder, he caught her gaze in their reflection.

"Nothing. Just...happy I guess." Esmeralda stroked his forearm allowing the hair there to tickle her fingertips.

"Mmhmm..." He'd picked that up from her.

It made her giggle again because he even went down an octave at the end the same way she did. Turning in his embrace, she lifted onto her tiptoes to capture his lips. Pulling away before the kiss went too far, she tapped his chest.

"I just need to put on my boots, then we can lace up your cuffs."

"Grrr!"

Swatting at him, she quirked an eyebrow. "Don't you growl at me. I was content to go by myself. You're the one who volunteered to be the Queen's guard."

"Yeah, but that was before I knew I'd have to walk around wearing nothing but a loin cloth."

"Stop being dramatic. You're wearing more than a loin cloth." Holding up the armbands, she started lacing one onto his left arm.

"Oh yeah...I'm practically dressed for winter now." Xavier quipped when she was done affixing the arm bands and wrist cuffs as part of his cosplay as one of Queen Neferata's royal guards.

"Stop being a baby. You look amazing."

"I'm half naked."

"Yeah, but the best half is still hidden." Esmeralda kissed him then pulled back. She stared at him with a finger tapping her chin in contemplation.

"I may need to amend my statement, because those legs are legging."

"That's it. I'm putting on pants." Xavier turned toward the closet and she latched onto his arm.

"Okay. Okay. I'll stop teasing. You really do look amazing. I'm going to be the envy of all the cosplay girlies and probably a good number of the guys as well."

Slipping her arms around his waist, she pressed her body as close to his front as possible. "I'm okay with them admiring the view, so long as they know this queen doesn't share."

Xavier's arms wrapped around her keeping her pressed against him. "Mmm...Just make sure the guys and the girls know it goes both ways...I don't share either."

Dipping low, he seized her lips in a drugging kiss. Heat skated over Esmeralda's skin and she moaned—partly from enjoyment and partly in regret. If she didn't put a stop to it, they'd be late. She didn't want to be at the back of the line to get her pictures with the creators of her favorite comic.

Tapping Xavier's chest, she was finally able to separate from the sensual promise of his kiss. They'd definitely revisit that subject. Later.

~

It was just as Esmeralda thought. Xavier was a huge hit at the Con. Between his towering height, his physique, and the scowl he wore, he made an excellent Royal Guard to her Queen Neferata. He even went so far as to bar people from getting close to her for pictures until she granted permission for them to approach.

It was amazing. By far, it was the most fun she'd had at a Con. Her fellow geeks were practically foaming at the mouth over Xavier. But, Esmeralda's measurement of enjoyment wasn't due to others being envious. It was because Xavier shed his tough guy persona for her. He geeked out right along with her when the actress featured on the cover of the Queen Neferata comic pulled Esmeralda close for a picture.

Dominique Truman was changing the game for actresses. She didn't fit the stereotype being an extra curvy, dark-skinned, African American woman who wore her natural hair. She went against the grain of the fair-skinned, super thin starlets that had been pushed out as the blueprint. Dominique was showing the world the real blueprint, and Esmeralda was beyond stoked to meet her and have the actress complement her cosplay.

Xavier stood by proudly while Esmeralda took pictures with Dominique and the other actors. When they attempted to pull him into the photos, he hung back until she tugged him in next to her. She didn't miss the numerous cards being pressed into his hand and offers for modeling gigs. He was polite, but she knew he wouldn't call them.

During one of their many talks, he'd told her about his time on the natural body building circuit and how he'd accepted modeling gigs on the side to make ends meet until he'd amassed a big enough nest egg to give it up.

When they exited the venue, Esmeralda's face lit up with a bright smile. A small group of Xavier's Sin City brothers were parked directly in front on their motorcycles and wearing their cuts. The hoots and catcalls were reserved for Xavier, but their presence gave her a tingling feeling. Although they ribbed him, it was a show of support—like a family.

They were rough and definitely as tough as they appeared, but they had each other's back. For an only child like herself, found family was all she had in the way of siblings. Xavier had revealed the loss of his older brother at a young age. So, the Sinners filled the space for him. Instead of one brother, he had many. Each ready to roll out with him whenever he needed them.

Once the cellphones came out and the camera flashes started, Xavier was ready to put an end to their little gathering.

"Alright that's enough, assholes. Get the fuck out of here."

"But I thought you wanted me to braid your hair." Fubar called out with a huge grin on his face.

"Fuck off." Xavier growled.

"Aww...Toad, don't be like that. You'll look pretty." Fubar continued to tease.

"Keep talking shit and I'll braid *your* hair, alright." Xavier groused.

"Ooo... Can you do the designs with the flowers?" Fubar held his hands to his chest reminiscent of a teenage girl.

"Be glad I'm not in the mood to kick your ass."

Trick chuffed at Xavier's comment. "Thank God. That piece of scrap you have on barely covers your goods. I'm okay not being traumatized."

"You know what? Fuck all of y'all."

Amid laughter, Xavier flipped them the middle finger, wrapped an arm around Esmeralda's shoulders, and guided her to where they left his truck.

Chapter Twenty-Three

"Mmmm..."

Esmeralda moaned and attempted to squirm away from the intense, pulsating, pleasure Toad delivered. Grinning, he used his grip on her thighs to pull her back down for him to devour her sweet pussy.

"What did I tell you about running from me?"

Diving back in, he latched on to her sensitive bundle of nerves, flicking it with his tongue exactly the way she liked. A few more licks and she released his reward amid keening wails. *Damn...*

Just hearing her cum made him hard as a brick, but tasting her juices put him in an agonizing conundrum. He wanted to have his fill of the decadent cream, but he also wanted to drive his cock inside her until he couldn't tell where he ended and she began. Opting for the former, he tightened his hold on her legs and drank of her essence.

Only when she was reduced to jerks and shudders did he rise to his knees stroking his shaft. As his fingers glided along his length, he stared at her as she watched him behind lowered lashes. She was fucking gorgeous and made more so by the loving glow she emitted. She probably didn't even realize she did it, but it turned his cock to granite whenever she looked at him the way she was right then.

Slipping his hands beneath her legs, he bent them at the knee. When he had her at the angle he wanted, he entered the warmth of her velvet walls. *Fuck!* Toad grit his teeth. The feeling of her wrapped around him did him in every time. Her lashes lifted as her fingers found his holding her legs and ghosted over them before traveling as far up his arms as she could reach.

With one final thrust he bottomed out in her honeyed core. He closed his eyes for a brief moment to lose himself completely in the feeling, but he couldn't keep them closed. He had to see his length plunging into her tightness. Simply seeing her puffy nether lips surrounding him was enough to make him blow his load, however he held on.

Toad's gaze went from where they were joined together back up her torso, lingering on her breast as they jiggled deliciously with each thrust, before landing on Esmeralda's face and those dark captivating eyes.

"Fuck, I love you, baby."

"Mmm...I love you too." She released the words in a satisfied slur which puffed out his chest. No matter how she said it or how many times, he craved hearing the words.

Pushing her legs until her knees where essentially next to her ears, he dipped low taking her lips in a scorching kiss. The new position gave him increased depth and when her channel clamped even tighter around his thickness, he nearly lost his mind. Without consulting him, his hips picked up a brutal rhythm.

Esmeralda's cries intensified and mingled with his groans and grunts as their bodies collided together in a timeless dance. Sweat dripped from his forehead as he fought to maintain control. Snatching the last of his resolve, Esmeralda's pussy convulsed around him as she reached her peak. Unable to hold on any longer, he followed her over the cliff releasing into her quivering channel.

Breathing heavily, he lowered her legs and reluctantly withdrew from her sheath. *Fuck the mouse*. Being inside Esmeralda was the happiest place on earth. Flopping next to her on the damp sheets, Toad appreciated the cool air drifting over his overheated body. Esmeralda's contented sighs were the best background music as they both came down from their orgasmic high.

As he lay there, simply enjoying the sound of them breathing in tandem Toad allowed his mind to drift. He thought of the way they met and how Esmeralda became important in his life so quickly. In biker timing, it was actually slow. They tended to move decisively when they wanted someone.

After the shitstorm that was the attempts to kidnap Esmeralda, Toad had stuck kind of close. He'd had to break away on occasion to help his brothers out or take care of something at Sin Gym, but otherwise, he stayed nearby.

He didn't consider Braxton Cartwright a threat. Unless ghosts were real, there was absolutely zero chance of him harming Esmeralda. As it turned out, the man was more than a little deranged. He thought he could scare Esmeralda into backing off of the case his sister-in-law brought to her company.

Once he found out she'd already completed her analysis, he thought he could get Esmeralda to invalidate her own findings and proclaim the woman he'd tried to pass off as his wife to be the real Melisandre Montague-Cartwright.

Unfortunately for him, even if he hadn't met with Toad's vengeance, the chick he had pretending to be his wife turned on him immediately when process servers showed up on the doorstep. This was a week after Cartwright's mysterious disappearance. She did everything but handstands to keep from being charged as an accessory to murder. Since the police couldn't find Cartwright, she was the next best choice.

Toad couldn't feel sympathy for her either. She'd knowingly posed as Melisandre Cartwright for access to the woman's wealth. But, a grifter's gonna grift. She was presently a guest of Alameda County.

The FBI agent who infiltrated their club posing as an Angel, Deena Hall, hadn't been quite as easily dispensed with as Braxton Cartwright. It turned out Esmeralda was correct. The agent had some pretty high up connections keeping her insulated. However, the Sinners had connections too.

Agent Hall had been busted down and sent out of California to ride a desk in some obscure office. Her life was spared, for the moment. But it was forfeit if she ever stepped foot inside a state with a Sin City MC chapter. It wasn't the ending Toad wanted. He'd live with it, though, as long as his brothers were safe from her dealings.

Levering himself from the bed, Toad went to the bathroom. Instead of their usual, he decided to run a bath. Esmeralda had insisted on wearing high stiletto-heeled platform boots with her costume. Those boots almost got her fucked in the truck, but he managed to wait until they got home. They inspired nasty thoughts, but they hurt her feet after so many hours. He knew she'd appreciate a hot bath instead of a warm towel.

As he walked back into the bedroom to get his woman, Toad stopped for a second to appreciate her in all of her well-fucked glory. She released a sigh as her eyes fluttered open to see him standing there.

"What?" Her raspy voice skated across him making his cock jerk. *Down boy.*

"Nothing, Princess Peach. Just admiring you."

"Mmm..." Esmeralda stretched causing the sheet to fall away from her full breasts. "If I'm a princess, does that make you my frog prince?"

Not bothering to go into the differences between toads and frogs, he scooped her into his arms. Then, he snagged a quick kiss. "How about you kiss me some more to see if I change?"

The End

Bonus Scene

Sign up for my newsletter to receive a bonus scene from ***Toad***.
https://sendfox.com/DarieMcCoy

All Books in the Sin City MC Oakland Chapter

Nitro

By Cassie Verano

Artyom

By Cam Johns

Calix

By Tonya Ink

Vex and Blue

By Shyla Colt

King

By Courtney Dean

Fubar

By Michel Prince

Ace

By Tameka Brown

Frenchie

By Niccoyan Zheng

Maximus

By L. Loren

Join our Facebook Group!

Sin City MC Clubhouse

Acknowledgments

I sincerely appreciate the Sin City MC family for welcoming me into the fold. A special thanks to Courtney Dean for allowing my characters to play in the world she built. It has been an awesome and rewarding experience. A special thank you to my readers for continuing to rock with me no matter which path I take. Your support means everything to me. As always, I thank my family and friends for their unwavering support of me on this writing journey.

About the Author

Darie McCoy is an independent author of contemporary, interracial, romantic suspense, and paranormal/shifter romance books. A reader first, she enjoys reading books across many genres although romance holds a special place in her heart. Her experience working in a STEM field offers her a unique perspective which she uses in each story she pens.

When she doesn't have her nose in a book or her fingers on the keyboard, Darie enjoys working in her vegetable garden. A serial hobbyist, she also enjoys knitting, sewing, baking and canning. One of her favorite treats to make is salted caramel popcorn. Amongst her friends, she's known to transport the sweet treat in large quantities to share whenever they get together.

Born and raised in the south, Darie stands by the staunchly held southern sentiments that the best tea is sweet tea and college football is life.

Also by Darie McCoy

Central Valley Pack Series

Chosen

Healed

Frost Family Series

For Real

Sano's Queen (A Novella)

Christmas Candy

Draft Pick Series

Draft Pick Season I: Carver

Draft Pick Season II: Andrei

Other books/stories

Involuntary

Just Kiss Me (Part of Cupid's Kiss Anthology)

Power (Loving Hearts Loving Day Anthology)

Made in the USA
Monee, IL
30 July 2023